Scorned
Twisted Tales of Familiar Faces
Z.S. Diamanti

M4L Publishing

For Gabe

Murky Waters

HERCULES CLAWED HIS FINGERS into the thick mud, searching for any way to keep himself from being dragged under the surface of the murky waters.

How did this go so wrong?

The hero grunted as the tentacle wrapped around his neck, squeezed tighter and pulled with greater force. If not for the immense muscles that bulged around his neck, he thought the tentacle might have already crushed his windpipe. Mud pressed between his fingers as he searched for something—anything—to slow him down, but the creature dragged him through the mud on his back, rendering his considerable strength nearly useless.

This wasn't the first nasty spot he'd been in, but he'd developed quite the distaste for Poseidon's monsters that lurked beneath murky surfaces. Mud oozed between his fingers and the back of his head sloshed into the water, sending chilled ripples down his spine as he choked against the tentacle clamping his throat.

Don't get distracted, he scolded himself.

His eyes darted from side to side, looking for his club. The swamp creature had caught him by surprise and knocked the weapon from his grasp as he was guiding their most recent damsel to his friend, Liamecles.

Where in Boreas did he get to?

"Liam—" Hercules tried to cry out, but could not get the name of his friend out of his mouth as the tentacle choked the air from his words.

And where was Iole? Or ... wait. Did she even come on this mission with them? Hercules' head swam like his mop of hair flowing away in the waters. His thoughts were static and fuzzy. His eyes narrowed as obsidian filled the edges of his vision. A vein bulged from his forehead and his neck muscles rippled as he wrenched with all his might to pull free.

Yet still, his fingers caught no hold in the slimy mud.

Murky water poured into his ears as he struggled to keep his mouth and nose above the surface. His arms twitched with rage as his feet flailed.

Hercules glanced about, looking for any sign of his companions, any last sight of them to put some hope back in his chest where the air had left his lungs empty. He saw no sign of them. In the forest's shadow, he saw nothing. Except ...

A pair of wicked, pale green eyes. He'd seen them before.

Hylas, his former armor bearer, and more importantly his friend, flashed through his mind. Hylas had been young, strong, handsome, and far smarter than Hercules himself. The armor bearer had the entire world ahead of him. Hercules knew that the man had a great destiny ahead of him; he knew it in his bones. Until that Fates-cursed *Argo* mission. It was supposed to be the greatest mission of the Age. Heroes from all over Greece had gathered together to embark on the quest for the Golden Fleece.

Alas, when he went to the spring to refill his pitcher, a water nymph pulled Hylas under, and no one ever saw the bright young man again.

Hercules had cut at the water like a lunatic. Hacking and slashing, kicking and cursing. He chased the streams through the forest, looking for the monster who took Hylas, but never found it. By the time he returned to the shore, the *Argo* was gone. Hercules had knelt at the edge of the forest and wept until he had no tears left to shed.

That's when he'd first seen the pale green eyes lurking in the shadows ...

If he could gasp at their presence now, he would have. Instead, his eyes widened, threatening to pop right out of their sockets. His jaw clenched so hard that his teeth ached as though they might shatter under the grimace. He released his lackluster grip on the bank and slipped under the water in less than a heartbeat.

Hercules grabbed at the tentacle around his throat as it lashed him about. If the lack of oxygen hadn't already depleted his ability to think rationally, he was sure the whipping motion and the murky bubbles produced by the monster would have disoriented him.

When Hercules couldn't rip the tentacle from his neck, he pulled at the length of it as though he were drawing in a rope. In desperation, he squeezed the tentacle in both hands and bit down hard. His jaw popped under the immense pressure and putrid ichor filled his mouth. But it worked. The tentacle writhed away through the milky depths.

Hercules flailed in an attempt to reorient himself in the water, trying to find the surface. Only the barest glimmer of light above him refracted through the swamp water, but it was there. He pulled and kicked, swimming as fast as his oxygen-deprived muscles could move his massive form.

His hand broke the surface. But the creature was quick in its own element.

Another tentacle wrapped around Hercules' ankle, halting him just before his face could break out into the refreshing forest air.

Pressure built up around his eyes and his lungs burned, ready to burst. There was no air, only cloudy waters surrounding him. Hercules imagined Hylas in a similar situation all those years ago. He imagined how the young man must have been terrified. He imagined the waters filling the armor bearer's lungs and drowning out the hope of any bright future ahead.

Hercules didn't see any bright future for himself in drowning, but he also couldn't hold his breath anymore. His body convulsed against his efforts. He had no choice. He had to breathe.

Suddenly, a spear sliced through the water next to him, planting itself into the tentacle that wrapped around his ankle. The monster released him, and a sonorous shriek shook the surrounding water.

Hercules gasped and coughed as he gulped the forest air. He swirled his arms and legs wearily, not sure if he was going toward solid ground.

"You dropped your club," a familiar voice said nearby.

Hercules clambered to all fours in the mud before sitting back on his heels to look up at his friend. "Nice of you to drop in," he rasped, his voice hoarse.

Iole stood above him, glimmering spear in hand. "Oh, well, if you have this handled, I can always keep looking for Ellysia. Plenty of Skuld Mire to wade through."

"No," Hercules grunted with an upraised hand, still catching his breath. "We found her. Liamecles has her."

"Oh, good," Iole elongated the second word. "So, this is just some recreational sport?"

Just then, the creature burst from the surface of the swamp, whirling and shaking its tentacles to make itself big and scary.

"Marsyas' breath!" Iole cursed. "He's sure ugly. Where'd he come from?"

Hercules grunted and grabbed the club Iole had planted upright in the mud before him. He had no idea where the monster came from. How many had he fought without ever knowing their origin?

Though, after seeing the eyes in the shadows, he couldn't help but wonder if there was more to this encounter. He'd made plenty of enemies along the way to becoming "Greece's Greatest Hero." Hercules spat swamp muck from his mouth. He'd angered kings and monsters, titans and demigods. Any number of them could be out to kill him.

But this was no time to think about such things. And Hercules was never much good at thinking with anything other than his fists, anyway. His knuckles whitened as he gripped the club, its surface ornamented with carved pictographs of his own deeds. His teeth ground together, threatening to crack inside his mouth.

Without a word, he launched himself at the writhing creature, bludgeoning tentacles with such force they fell limp to the waters below.

Meanwhile, a pair of eyes blinked and disappeared into the shadows of the verdant forest.

The Monster

THE STENCH THAT PERMEATED the taverna in the backwater town of Laspe forced short involuntary bursts of air out of Hercules' recoiling nostrils. He'd smelled far worse, of course, but the ever-present stench in the place made him feel as though he were sitting in squalor. The cup of swill the locals called ale did little to make the place feel more homey. But with Laspe being the only town this close to the Skuld Mire, he and his companions had few options. This was made even more evident by the fact that the place was full of patrons, all with nowhere else to go for a drink.

Hercules grunted and downed the contents of his cup before clacking it back on the bar top. He grimaced as a fissure grew in the side of the clay cup and split it entirely. Often, even when he was trying to have a quiet evening to recover, his mighty strength made him feel like a raging bull—a side effect of his lineage.

Thank you, Zeus, he thought sarcastically. He'd never had much love for the god who'd sired him. Especially knowing that Zeus had tricked his mother by appearing in the form of her husband, Amphitryon, the man Hercules really called father. The tales of Zeus' exploits with human women were renowned, and Hercules wondered how many women the god had tricked.

Foamy suds wet Hercules' hand, and he realized the clay cup rested in pieces in his grip. With an apologetic half-smile, he pulled the last coin from his pocket to slide it over to the taverna owner, but the little old man waved it away and produced another from behind the bar, filling it with his "finest ale." Hercules sighed. He left the coin on the bar top anyway, and leaned back on his stool, stretching his massive arms up and backward to loosen the muscles in his back. The big man ran his hands through his dark, wavy hair. Despite being rinsed twice, the strands still felt grimy.

Hercules slumped over, resting his forearms on the bar again, and took the fresh cup in both hands to handle it with care. He looked between his newly filled cup and the cracked one, oozing the foamy remnants of ale. Hercules felt like the broken cup—battered, used, and cracked under the impossible weight of this life. He imagined most children of the gods of Olympus felt that way. He didn't recall many stories where they'd experienced lives of peace and prosperity. Being a son of the preeminent god of the pantheon didn't line up the stars any better for Hercules. Instead, it seemed to place a target on his back. And he knew he wasn't the only one. Zeus had sown his wild oats far and wide. How many others hid their lineage?

Hercules never had a choice in the matter. Even from a young age, his strength betrayed his heritage. As a babe when he lay in his crib, two serpents had wriggled in to kill him and his brother in the middle of the night. Hercules, though small in stature, took the snakes by the throat and choked them out with his might. No, he never stood a chance of hiding his pedigree.

He'd often wondered how his life might look if he had hidden his mighty strength. Could he have been a general like his adopted father, Amphitryon? He and his brother Iphicles leading the warriors of Thebes to vanquish their enemies, coming home to their mother, Alcmena, who wove intricate arrays of blankets in worry while she awaited their return. Would they return to their wives and children, running to greet them in the field before they could even reach the doors?

A lump grew in Hercules' throat, and he tried to swallow it down. His cheeks wrinkled and burned as his nostrils flared. A single tear rolled from his eye, navigating the rough skin on his face before disappearing into his beard. *Meg…*

He wiped his face with his enormous paw of a hand and downed the ale in his new cup. This time, he grabbed his club as if to give him the strength not to smash the cup as he set it down on the bar top.

The cup cracked anyway.

No. A normal life had never been in the stars for him. He imagined that no matter how the gods' blood manifested itself in their offspring, eventually the curse would be discovered. The only one he'd ever known to find some sort of peace was Theseus. Only because he was the wisest and most compassionate man Hercules had ever met. But eventually, even Theseus fell prey to the gods and their games, landing himself somewhere in the depths of Hades.

Even though he wished it deep within his belly, Hercules wasn't sure it was possible for any demigod to keep it hidden and live a normal life.

Cheers filled the taverna as another patron entered the room with flair.

Liamecles smiled and waved, Ellysia hanging warily on his arm.

Hercules emitted an unintended growl as he turned back to the barkeep, who was already filling a new clay cup.

"Another one for you, sir," the little old man said, his white whiskers bobbing as he blinked nervously and wiped the sweat from his brow.

Hercules nodded and tried to return the gesture with a kind smile, but realized his gritted teeth probably looked more like a scowl.

"Thank you," a quiet voice said to the barkeep as the old man scurried away to serve the rambunctious crowd gathering around Liamecles for a tale about how he rescued the fair princess, Ellysia, from the swamp beast. Iole leaned on the bar next to Hercules, her glimmering bracers catching the firelight that illuminated the taverna in an amber glow. "He sure knows how to make an entrance," Iole said, shaking her head as she took a sip of her own cup.

"Would have been nice of him to 'make an entrance' while that monster was dragging me through the mud," Hercules grumbled, not looking over at the other man. He didn't need to. He could see it all clearly from his seat as he slumped over the bar. Liamecles and his curly golden locks. His square jaw shaved clean. The princess clinging to her dashing rescuer's muscular arms and lean form. Hercules had seen it a dozen times before.

"I'll have a talk with him," Iole said with a sigh.

"What's the point?"

"The point is, you don't leave one of your friends to die. Ever. You, of all people, know that. You've told him as much yourself."

"And how many times must we tell him this?" Hercules mocked. He thumbed his club, a tic that had formed over the years. The veins on his immense arms bulged as he squeezed. It wasn't Iole's fault. And in truth, he had told Liamecles to get Ellysia to safety. Hercules had merely thought the younger man would have come running back to the fight once he'd gotten the woman out of harm's way. Having seen the beauty of the fair princess later, Hercules understood why Liamecles had been ... preoccupied. All the long years they'd traveled together, Liamecles had always had a soft spot for the prettier damsels.

"As many times as it takes to get it through his thick, chiseled skull," Iole said nonchalantly.

"No," Hercules sighed the word. "He kept Ellysia safe, and we killed whatever that monstrosity was that Poseidon cooked up in the bog."

"You think the creature was the work of Poseidon?"

"Who else?" Hercules asked, his gaze now leaving his intricately carved club to read his friend's face.

"Though it lurked in the waters of the bog, it seemed ..." She paused for a moment, pursing her lips and scrunching her nose as she thought. "Unnatural. Have you ever seen the like?"

Hercules said nothing at first, his mind remembering only the pale green eyes that haunted the shadows of the swamp forest. A pang of eerie familiarity shuddered through him. Not that he knew the eyes or could even make out their details, for they were always shrouded in an aura, but the eyes had been present at so many horrifying events in his life. "No. I haven't," he said, suddenly remembering Iole awaited an answer.

"Hercules?" a voice slurred over the excited crowd, which fell to sudden whispers.

Hercules' massive shoulders tensed. A low growl rolled through him.

"Easy ..." Iole whispered to him and placed a staying hand on his forearm.

"Isn't he the one who tamed Pegasus?" the drunkard warbled.

"No, that was Bellerophon, you dolt," another patron jeered.

"Whatever ..." the drunk said. Though Hercules hadn't turned to face the crowd, he could tell the drunk's voice drew closer. "So ... You're the one who cut off the head of Medusa?"

"Wrong again." This time it was Liamecles who corrected him. "That was his cousin Perseus."

"Oh, righ—" the drunk started to say, but hiccupped. "Son of Zeus, right? Like Ares and Hephaestus' brother, and what's the goddess' name? Heb ... Heb something?"

"Half-brother," a younger man in the crowd shouted, excited to join in on the corrections.

"Oh ... not even a full god ... The Minotaur slayer?" This time his words were less confident and directed back toward Liamecles.

"That was Theseus ... a dear friend ..." Liamecles said, a somber note in his timbre.

"Then wha did you dooo?" the man slurred. "Doesn't sound like the Greatest Hero of Greece to me."

Hercules winced as the rest of the taverna fell silent. He hated when people called him that. Most of the time, he didn't feel like a hero. He had done so many horrible things. Most of the time he felt like a—

"Wait a minute ..." the drunk started. Hercules' broad knuckles whitened as his grip tightened on his club. "You're the one who abandoned the *Argo* and her crew. The greatest mission of the Ag—"

As fast as lightning, Hercules was on his feet. As he swirled, his stool went flying to the side and clattering to the floor. His mighty frame loomed over the drunk. Heaving breaths bobbed Hercules' wide shoulders as his muscles rippled with furious tension.

Iole swiftly moved to his side. "Watch your tongue, fool. Marsyas' breath! You know not who you speak to."

Rage flashed through Hercules, his eyes red with malicious intent.

Iole broke the terrified silence. "He did not abandon the *Argo*. His armor bearer was torn from him, stolen away by a water nymph. A monster."

He doesn't deserve to hear this story, Hercules fumed inside. *He doesn't deserve to hear Hylas' name.*

"My friends," Liamecles cut in. "This is Hercules. Slayer of the Nemean lion. Slayer of the nine-headed Hydra. Capturer of the fire-breathing Ceryneian Hind. The ..."

Hercules barely heard his friend as the blood boiled within him. Depictions of all twelve labors he'd conducted under the service of King Eurystheus were intricately carved in the club, a parting gift from one of the most talented artists of Mycenae. They were all there. The Erymanthian boar. The Augean Stables. The Stymphalian birds. The Cretan bull. The mares of Diomedes. All of them. But none of that mattered. The club rested easily in his fist, an extension of his arm, as though it were a part of him.

"... the girdle of Hippolyta, queen of the Amazons. That's a story not to be missed," Liamecles said with a chuckle and a playful wink. The weight of the room was thinning as the crowd listened in awe and Liamecles entertained them with the list of Hercules' labors. "Snatcher of the cattle of the three-headed giant, Geryon. Collector of the golden apples of the lovely Hesperides," he said with a wiggle of his brows and a charming grin. "I would have been very helpful on that mission." The patrons laughed.

"And finally," Liamecles said, taking a breath as though the labors were an endeavor merely to list, "the capturer of Cerberus. The most vile and horrifying monster from the depths of Hades."

Hercules took a slow step forward, looming over the drunken man who had started this whole affair. Iole motioned to stop him, but pulled her hand back tentatively.

"He forgot to mention *madman*, destroyer of all who get in his way," Hercules growled to the drunk. Not a soul in the place would have argued it, by the look in the demigod's eyes. "Slayer of kings. Slaughterer of towns." Hercules took another slow step toward the man, looming an entire head and shoulders above him. A puddle grew on the floor as the man, visibly shaking, wet the front of his linen chiton.

A snarl rose from inside Hercules as he leaned in. "Do you know why they send me to slay the monsters and beasts of your nightmares?"

The man shook his head, almost imperceptibly, with his entire body shivering.

"Because to all of them, I am the monster."

Sentimental

HERCULES STOOD QUIETLY ON the cliff overlooking the sea. The breeze blew gently through his mop of hair and caressed his face with a kind coolness. His hands stretched open to feel the golden heads of grain that playfully batted at him. He took a deep breath, feeling the air work its way into his lungs and energizing his blood. A hint of peace teased at him. He closed his eyes, leaving the sight of the sea behind for a vision of a lost past.

Megara laughed and danced with one of his sons, Theo. Luka and Alkaios jumped around, parrying and dodging each other's sticks in a play sword fight. It had been a glorious day, just like this one. The sun shone and a soothing sea breeze kept them cool. The joy on his family's faces that day warmed something inside him.

Warmth ... fire ...

Suddenly, a nightmarish scene flashed in his memory. Hercules gripped a head of grain in his hand, pulverizing it. In his mind, he beat back the fragmented memory that plagued him. Every time it invaded his mind, it appeared shattered, as though he were looking at a mirror that had crashed to the ground. Blood everywhere. The limp forms of his children ... Megara ... Blood dripping from his own hands. He'd killed them all. He didn't know why or remember how, but the blood of his family was on his hands. Their home, a burning carcass, raged with fire, nothing but the skeletal remains radiating heat as the flames licked hungrily.

He remembered little more about that night; his memory broken like his heart. He was told he killed his own family in a bout of madness, though he couldn't reconcile it as possible. But the events of that night were nothing more than a blank in his mind. The only explanation must be the truth, regardless of his disbelief at the possibility that he would have been capable of slaying his family.

Hercules bellowed a great roar over the sea far below. Birds scattered from the field all about, squawking and chittering in consternation. A golden head of grain thwapped against his fist. Hercules opened his hand and closed his eyes again, hoping to get one last glimpse of that long ago happy memory of his family, vibrant and alive. He squeezed his eyes shut, but no vision came. He sighed, but just before he opened his eyes, a cool breeze brushed across his face—perhaps a gift from Aeolus, King of the Winds—and with it, a flickering moment from that day.

Soft footsteps waded through the field behind him, but Hercules did not turn toward the noise.

"Where is Hercules, the Greatest Hero of Greece?" Hercules did not flinch at the old man's words—his voice soothing and carrying a compassionate air.

"In a dream," Hercules whispered.

"Ah, and what dream is that?"

Hercules sighed again, the wind taking his breath and blowing it across the sea. For a moment longer, he stared at the back of his eyelids, the sun painting them bright red. Finally, he turned to his old friend, Admetus. The man's wispy white hair swirled and flourished on top of his head. As he'd aged, the man had grown shorter and slighter, making him appear a mere quarter of Hercules' enormous size.

"Ah," Admetus said with a knowing nod. "I often think of Alcestis …" his words choked off. He cleared his throat before continuing. "She used to stand right over there at sunrise. She loved to watch the sun peek over the edge of the sea, turning the world pink and orange. Occasionally, she'd catch me watching her, and she'd turn her brilliant smile on me, brighter than the sun. No matter how old we got, she remained as beautiful as ever."

Hercules swallowed the lump forming in his throat. He could imagine it. Admetus' villa by the sea was of impeccable beauty. Hercules had found refuge and rest there many times as Admetus and Alcestis were gracious hosts and kind friends. Admetus' position as a respected elder and former member of the king's council in the nearby city of Pherae had afforded him great wealth and honor. Hercules could never repay the man's generosity. Though he felt deeply indebted to Admetus, Hercules could not keep himself from coming back to the warm place. It was the closest thing he felt to home anywhere in Greece.

Though that had not always been the case...

"Her loss …" Admetus hesitated. "Well, you know what that loss feels like."

Hercules merely grunted and nodded his understanding. He knew.

"But I'm an old man, never to find love again. Not as strapping as a young man like you," the old man said, giving Hercules a light punch on his big arm.

Hercules huffed a laugh and shook his head. "Just because I'm not ancient like you doesn't mean I'm a young man. I feel it in my bones. A fatigue that fills me to the core."

"You know what can fix that?"

Hercules sighed. "Don't say love."

"Love," Admetus said with emphasis.

"I have a wife," Hercules said flatly.

"Ah yes. An arranged marriage for the political machinations of Grecian city states. How romantic."

Hercules rolled his eyes. The two men stood on the cliffside in silence for a long moment, listening to the crashing waves far below.

"How is Deianira, anyway? And the children?" Admetus asked, more solemnly.

"Well," Hercules said. "Alive."

"And that's all that matters," Admetus said with a hint of disapproval edging his words. "When was the last time you saw them?"

"A year ..." the big man stopped. Had it only been a year? "Maybe more."

The old man turned his gray eyes upon him, a pained look on his face.

"Don't look at me like that, Admetus," Hercules said, throwing his hands in the air. "I have done my duty to her. It's the same thing they've all wanted. She has four children with the blood of the gods coursing through their veins. She got what she wanted."

"Is that all she wanted?"

"Of course it was!" Hercules had convinced himself that it was. Though, as he said it to Admetus, he didn't sound so convincing. He doubled down. "Just like the rest of them. Every other week, I hear of some new woman claiming to have birthed a son or daughter of Hercules."

In truth, those claims would have been more reasonable years prior. When he was a young hero, adventuring and rescuing damsels and saving cities from monsters and winning battles alongside his brother Iphicles, he had sown his wild oats—a characteristic he'd likely acquired from his father, Zeus, but one he now avoided like the plague. But when he was young, he was more given to the passions of the moment, not realizing the ulterior motives of the women that threw themselves at him. He did not doubt that many of those claims from his younger years were likely true. He had no way to refute them. But all that had changed when he'd met Megara. He'd done right by her ... until the nightmare ...

"And the children?" Admetus asked, no judgment in his words.

Though the old man's words bore no condemnation, the question stung. Every time Hercules had gone to visit them, he saw the light of hope in their eyes and a love welled up within him. But he couldn't feel that way. What right did he have? After everything he'd done ...

"You know they're better off without me. They're safe. Deianira is safe." Hercules' words got quieter as he spoke. "I can never be with anyone like that again. You know that."

"That is unfortunate," Admetus said, placing a comforting hand on Hercules' forearm. "I only want to see your life filled with joy again. And I know I'm not the only one."

Hercules looked up, realizing who Admetus implied. Iole stood on the cliff a short distance away. The sea breeze blew her wavy honey-brown hair with effortless beauty. Her athletic form was accentuated by the linen chiton that flitted around her. Her attractiveness was undeniable. Hercules knew that in his younger years, he would have been smitten with the woman. But he didn't allow himself to see her that way now. They'd been traveling together for a few years now, slaying monsters and saving cities. His name got much of the hype, but he was merely pressing on and doing anything he could to make recompense for what he'd done.

"Maybe in another life ..." he whispered.

"Well, my friend, this is the only one you get. I don't want you to forget to live it. Otherwise, you'll find yourself on the side of a cliff, looking out over the sea all by yourself with broken memories. The funny thing about memories is, they don't always show us the truth of a scene, but rather a version, colored by the feelings that were reared in the moment. Have you considered going to Olympus to get the gods' help with fixing your memory?"

"No mortal can go to Olympus. You know that."

"Do you count?"

Hercules chuckled and shook his head. "I would have to accomplish one of the greatest feats in the history of all Greece to even get consideration for an audience with the gods of Olympus. And even then, I *still* might not be able to wash away what I've done."

"None of us can wash away what we've done," Admetus said. "We can only do our best moving forward to leave a better legacy for those to come."

"You're getting sentimental in your old age," Hercules said with a smirk.

"And you're getting grumpy." Admetus laughed. "I can only imagine what magnificent feat you will accomplish to get an audience with the gods. I'm sure it will be marvelous."

Hercules shook his head, not terribly convinced. Though the idea sparked something within him. Perhaps that was his next step. Maybe he wouldn't be overwhelmed by guilt if he could get his memory fixed... But there was also the chance that clearing his memory would only clarify his condemnation.

"But tonight, King Linos is looking forward to thanking you for saving his daughter, Ellysia. You are lucky I convinced him to let me host the banquet here."

Lucky. Hercules chuckled, but he was grateful for the old man.

Alone in a Crowded Room

Torches danced in their sconces, flickering in rhythm with the band that played in the corner of the great hall. Dancers twirled in the open area, shaking the beads on their skirts and beating tambourines. King Linos had spared no expense for the celebration. Every kind of luxury food Hercules had ever seen was heaped on Admetus' guest table. Hercules picked at an eel on the table in front of him. He'd already eaten his fill, despite his lackluster appetite.

Nearby, Admetus sat on his pillow next to King Linos. The old man had positioned himself between Hercules and the king—a kind gesture as Admetus took up the mantle of engaging the king and matching his merriment. Hercules watched for much of the night. Like most kings, when a celebration was warranted, he had plenty of friends who would show up for free food and a good time. Plus, when given the opportunity to see Hercules, Greatest Hero of Greece, few people denied the invitation.

As much as it annoyed him, the buzz of the banqueters distracted him from the quiet sorrow he'd be drinking away in his room. Though there were dozens of people in the banquet hall, he couldn't help but feel utterly alone.

In the old days, women lurked in the wings, looking for opportunities to try their luck at seduction. Men would chance an encounter, just so they could say they shook the hand of Hercules. He must have looked particularly grumpy, or the torches cast ominous shadows around his mountainous frame, because tonight, none approached.

In fairness, Liamecles had gotten quite adept at shielding him from the crowds, drawing them to himself with stories and that perfect smile. Even now, the princess Ellysia clung to his arm. Hercules knew she'd be disappointed like so many other princesses had been when Liamecles eventually told her he must leave to save yet another town from their imminent doom. Though he would, of course, "carry her love in his heart as a reminder of their nights together."

A smirk crossed Hercules' face as he watched.

"Where is Hercules, the Greatest Hero of Greece?" Admetus spoke next to him, eyeing the big man with a soft smile.

"I am here, my friend," he said.

"Are you?"

Hercules chuckled and half turned toward his gracious host. King Linos was otherwise engaged with a pretty young woman who Hercules guessed was a front runner to become his new queen. The big man shook his head.

"I am. Just watching Liamecles. I don't know how he has the energy to keep the masses happy."

"Perhaps you *are* getting old," the old man mused.

Hercules barked a laugh.

"I seem to remember a much younger hero who enjoyed my wine a little too much and loved the attention of anyone who'd give it to him," Admetus said through a chuckle of his own.

The big man shrugged his assent, knowing the old man to be right. Liamecles reminded him so much of his younger self. It was hard to deny. Iole had asked Hercules once why he still brought Liamecles with him. While his skill with a blade, his uncanny knack for tracking down the subject of their pursuit, and his incredible attention to detail were the reasons he gave, Hercules could never quite explain the kinship he felt toward the other man. Perhaps he saw a bit of his old self in the man. Or maybe Liamecles reflected everything he wished he saw in himself.

"I seem to remember a younger, but still old, man who drank that wine with me," Hercules quipped. "Drank me under the table a few times, if I recall."

"A few times?" Admetus reared back, his brows furrowing.

"Alright," Hercules laughed. "Every time."

Wrinkles bunched up around the old man's eyes as Admetus smirked. "Well, one day you're enjoying the prime of your life with good friends and the woman you love. The next she's gone, and you can sit in a room crowded with people and still feel alone." Hercules nodded solemnly, reading the sorrow on the old man's face as he squinted it away to present a jovial host mask. "But we can't get them back. It is the way of things. Instead, we turn our eyes to what we leave behind. Have you given more thought to the grand feat you could accomplish to really get the attention of the gods?"

In truth, he had. But with all the things he'd already done in his life, he was having a hard time thinking of anything that would be grander. As much as he hated the "Greatest Hero of Greece" moniker, he had a history of accomplishments that dwarfed most other heroes' lives. Sitting with his old friend, however, only reinforced the idea he'd started plotting. If he was going to get to Olympus, where they could heal his shattered mind, and he could finally know what truly happened the night he killed his family, he'd have to do something truly heroic.

This Should Be Fun

"HADES?" LIAMECLES EXCLAIMED. HE wiped his face and shook a decanter of wine as if to test it before deciding it was good enough, then poured the contents into a clay cup. "It's too early for this."

"Why Hades?" Iole asked. "To most, it is a death sentence."

"I've been there before," Hercules stated plainly.

"Pah!" Liamecles laughed. "I know you hardly remember it because you slipped into a coma for weeks while I patched you up, but the last time you went there, Cerberus nearly ended you. Or have the scars disappeared on this giant pec of yours?" he asked, poking Hercules in the chest with an outstretched finger.

Hercules ran his hand over his chest. He could still feel the raised ridges of the giant scars that Cerberus, Hades' three-headed hound, had left. Liamecles was right. People remembered the story of his capture of Cerberus with marvel and wonder, but he'd been a bloody mess.

"I have not forgotten."

"Oh good! Then we're making a calculated decision to throw our lives away." Liamecles downed the contents of his cup.

Hercules growled.

"Hercules," Iole cut in again. "Why Hades?"

The hulking man took a deep breath and explained. "All these things I've done to make the world better. All these monsters I've slain. None of them have done a thing to atone for ..." His words trailed off. He couldn't finish that statement. He redirected. "I need to get the gods' attention. I need to do something they can't ignore. Something that will get me an audience in Olympus. I know if I can do that, someone there will be able to help me fix my memory. The worst part about what happened ..." No. There were a lot of worse parts about that night. He exhaled. "I just can't remember."

"It was a bout of madness," Liamecles said, his tone strangely compassionate. The man had a penchant for shifting his attitude. Sometimes he could be so bombastic, rallying people to their cause. And other times he could quietly meet a person in their darkest moments, extend a hand, and pull them back from the brink of destruction. "Theseus told me how some creatures have the ability to curse others with magic. You were struck by a curse from some monster or demigod or sorcerer you'd scorned."

Hercules chewed the inside of his mouth, processing what his friend had said. Theseus had told him the same thing after the slaughter of his family. Hercules had struggled to believe it was possible. The love he'd had for his family ... He'd thought it unbreakable. And if a love like that could be so idly tossed aside with some curse of madness ...

The pale green eyes invaded his mind. Who had he scorned so badly they would follow him like a wraith everywhere he went? Certainly, he'd made his fair share of enemies over the years, but the eyes held a great hatred he couldn't quite understand. Had the eyes been there that night? If only he could remember.

"Theseus was one of the wisest men of all Greece," Iole said in agreement. "And one of our greatest heroes."

"He still is," Hercules said.

"Is he though?" Liamecles asked, raising his hands quickly before the bristling Hercules. "He's trapped on a seat of forgetfulness in the bowels of the Underworld. A place—I would remind you—that shifts and changes like the waves of the sea. Just because you've been there once doesn't mean it will look the same to you. And besides, you never made it as far as Hades' palace in Tartarus. You encountered Cerberus so early in your descent. Oh, and that's another thing. What if Cerberus kills you properly this time?"

"Then it will finally be over!" Hercules snapped.

Iole and Liamecles both fell silent and stared at him. Hercules cursed himself. *Fool. That's not the way to convince them of your plan.*

Liamecles stepped to Hercules' side and placed a hand on his large shoulder. "Just because you don't feel like you have anything to lose, doesn't mean we have nothing to lose. You're a brother to me. You know I'll follow you anywhere, but I don't want to lose you. And I won't risk that without a truly remarkable reason."

Hercules heaved a sigh. "I'm sorry," he started again. "This will work. I know it will. It has to."

"You think rescuing Theseus is enough to get the gods' attention? I see how defying Hades will certainly get his," Iole reasoned.

"Theseus is one of Greece's most beloved heroes," Hercules said. Theseus had always been wiser and led with compassion. He was a good friend and mentor to many. The people of Greece, and especially Athens, loved him. "But we won't just be defying Hades."

Liamecles perked up from the corner of the room. Hercules knew he was on the right track. His friend had always had a rebellious attitude toward the gods of Olympus.

"Remember when Admetus hosted Apollo for a time because he was having a disagreement with Zeus?" Hercules asked.

"When are the gods not having a spat?" Liamecles scoffed.

"You mean before Alcestis died ..." Iole said, trying to keep the line of thought going.

"Right. When Apollo was here with him, he told Admetus that the Fates had spun out his thread and warned him of his impending death. Apollo said, if Admetus could find a willing substitute, someone could die in his place. You know Admetus though, he would never ask someone else for such a sacrifice. Unfortunately, Alcestis overheard their conversation and volunteered herself without his knowledge."

"Are you saying what I think you're saying?" Liamecles asked.

"We're going to get Alcestis back from the Underworld as well."

A brief silence swept over the room. Iole's lips pursed in thought and Liamecles crinkled his brow.

"So, let me get this straight," Liamecles said, pacing the marble floor. "You want to free one of the greatest heroes of Greece from the clutches of Hades, who likely won't be thrilled about it? But we all know Hades is not in everybody's good graces in Olympus. So just in case that's not enough, you also want to rip Alcestis from Death's grasp, defying a deal struck by Apollo. Thus, we defy both Olympus' renegade and its golden boy at the same time. Two for the price of one." He paused and his brows popped. "That's a pretty good deal ..." he mumbled.

"And with the added benefit of returning Alcestis to Admetus," Hercules added. "Though my heart wills me forward, purely to see our old friend filled with joy once more, it also has the potential to capture the attention of Aphrodite. The goddess of love surely won't miss such a touching reunion."

"Defy two gods, but make one happy," Liamecles grumbled. "I knew there'd be a catch."

"I've had a hard time coming up with another mission that would bring us such attention," Hercules said honestly.

"No, no," Liamecles waved it off. "I like it. I'm in."

The two men shifted their gaze to Iole, who'd fallen rather quiet.

"What about you?" Hercules asked.

"I don't know," she said. "Such a task comes with great dangers." Hercules deflated.

"But," she continued, "it comes with the potential for glorious reward."

"Yes," Hercules agreed. "It may be my best shot."

"Or it may be your doom," Iole said plainly.

"Wow. Optimistic," Liamecles quipped.

"Realistic," she retorted. "Have you considered seeing the oracle at Delphi about it?"

An involuntary snarl raised part of Hercules' lip. "No. I'll never talk to that witch again. She was the one who told me to indenture myself to Eurytus." Iole shifted uneasily. "The witch said he would give me tasks to complete for penance for what I did in my bout of madness. She was the one who said I needed to be purified before I'd find peace. Here I am, having completed more trials and missions than anyone ever expected, and years later, I still have no peace."

"Yeah ..." Liamecles said. "He doesn't like her. We don't bring her up."

"I would feel better with a prophetic word one way or the other," Iole confessed. Not having been with Hercules as long as Liamecles, nor having seen as much trouble as they'd wriggled themselves out of, she fell back to superstition rather easily.

"Oh, we'll get a sign," Hercules said.

"From whom?"

"On the path we travel, it's hard not to receive one," Hercules said.

"And what path is that?"

Hercules merely grinned.

"Oh," Liamecles said. "This should be fun."

Spartans

THE BAND OF SPARTAN mercenaries they had hired for the voyage spread out to find places to rest among the mighty oaks of Dodona. Hercules grunted as he walked by a few of the young Spartans, unrolling their gear to find some dried food. They looked as though they'd only seen eighteen or nineteen years, and Hercules was pretty sure they'd never been in an actual battle. For most of them, their beard scruff was patchy at best, not having grown into full maturity.

The mighty oaks of Dodona loomed heavily above them, casting shade upon them with a comforting grace. The long grass on the edge of the path swayed in the breeze, matching the wave of the tree branches. Dodona forest chirruped with lively critters, scurrying about, looking for food before night fell. Several nocturnal creatures sounded, having risen early for their night's hunt. It would almost have been a beautiful evening, if not for the grunts and joking among the mercenaries that milled around him.

It had always been easy to hire mercenaries for the missions that would present challenges for him on his own, or even with Liamecles' help. Iole had joined the two of them on their crusade to vanquish monsters after Hercules had torn down her father's house. The King Eurytus had been a liar and a cheat and had blamed Hercules for the death of his son. But like so many, the king's son, Eliarus, had been seeking adventure and glory and followed Hercules where only the mighty man could survive.

Though Hercules had expected Iole to hate him for it, she'd surprised him with understanding, hating the greed and venom that poured from her father's lying lips. Beyond that, she had proven herself to be far more cunning, skillful, and honorable than her brother or her father. He'd initially been overprotective of her, not wanting her to join him and Liamecles, but Hercules quickly learned he couldn't hold her back if he tried.

As he walked past a small group of mercenaries, he wondered if they would make it home from this quest. Spartans were, at least, trained warriors from a young age. Their motives of glory and honor and coming home as heroes were the same as so many other young warriors who'd signed on to many of his quests, but Hercules preferred Spartans, knowing they'd been through intensive training.

"Where did you find this lot?" Hercules asked Liamecles as they caught up at a known well along the path.

"Oh, no. Don't blame these baby faces on me. Iole's the one who found them at the taverna in Chalcis. All young, wide-eyed, and ready to prove themselves heroes."

Hercules scowled and glanced over his shoulder toward Iole, who stood next to a large oak, speaking to the young band's leader. He wasn't much older than the others, but stood confidently before the warrior woman. Hercules smirked as he realized the young man spoke to her with a familiar air. "Seems their leader has taken quite a liking to her."

"Oh, is that what you see? Seems to me she's rather smitten herself," Liamecles teased.

"What …?" Hercules grumbled. He watched for a moment longer, Iole fiddling with her long braid as she spoke with the leader. His broad shoulders put him a league above the rest of the Spartans, but not as large as Liamecles, and certainly nowhere near as large as Hercules himself. The Spartan's straight jaw and black locks of hair gave him a dangerously handsome look, even with his slightly crooked nose, clearly having been broken in the past. In the time they'd traveled together, Hercules had never really noticed Iole engaged in any romance. She carried a rather conservative air about her. Could be that he'd just been oblivious, drowning out his own sorrows. "I see."

"Iole's entitled to some fun as well," Liamecles said with a shrug before downing more water and wiping his face on the wrappings around his wrists. "Aphrodite knows she could use some."

Hercules grunted again. Liamecles had always been a bit overzealous with the fun. Maybe he was rubbing off on Iole.

"Have you even spoken to him yet?" Liamecles asked.

"No," Hercules admitted. In truth, he rarely spoke directly with the mercenaries unless he needed to fire them up and prepare them for battle.

"You really ought to. He's not as bad as he looks."

Hercules heaved a sigh before taking the waterskin Liamecles held out for him. He took several long swigs and steeled himself. Talking to people wasn't really his forte. So much so, that he once stubbornly refused a debate with the river god Achelous, offering only to wrestle him. In the end, Achelous took the form of a bull and Hercules conquered him. It was the very contest that won him the hand of his wife, Deianira. The thought of the incident and Deianira's shocked response to his rescue pasted a smirk across his lips. *"You're more bullheaded than a river god in the form of a bull! How is that even possible?"*

"Here he is now," Iole said to the Spartan leader as Hercules approached.

Hercules shook away the memory.

The Spartan beat a fist to his chest and gave a slight bow. "Hercules, it is an honor to accompany you."

Strangely, the Spartan's lack of using the normal honorific "Greatest Hero of Greece" frustrated Hercules. He assumed Iole had mentioned he didn't care for it. Which he didn't. But what else had she told the Spartan?

"Spartan," Hercules grumbled.

"Oh, my deepest apologies. My name is Nikanor," the man said with another bow.

"Stop doing that," Hercules said.

Nikanor stood straighter, his eyes narrowed as he appraised the burly man before him. "As you wish. I only mean to express the honor my company feels to be a part of one of your noble quests."

Noble? Hercules thought. He wasn't really sure how noble it was. Perhaps reuniting Admetus and Alcestis was noble. And maybe even recovering Athens' favorite hero could be noble. But in truth, it was rather personal and aimed at his own gain. Hercules wanted to complete this mission so *he* could go to Olypmus. So *he* could get his memories fixed. So *he* could find peace. So *he* could know what really happened that night ...

"We'll see how you feel when it's all over," he grumbled to the Spartan.

Iole obviously sensed that Hercules was in a foul mood, because she cut in before the Spartan could respond. "Nikanor was just telling me of the months he spent in these woods fighting the tribes."

"Terrible monsters," Nikanor said. "It took us months to push them back to the hilly area of western Dodona."

"Good," Hercules said.

"Good?" Nikanor's handsome face scrunched. "We lost many good men to protect the cities on the edges of the great forest."

"I mean, it's good you have some actual fighting experience. Where we're going, you're going to need it."

With that Hercules turned to rejoin Liamecles as the man sought a secure place for them to take turns sleeping and standing guard.

"Sir," Nikanor said, an edge to his voice. "Though many of them look young, my men are Spartans through and through. They have trained their entire lives for a quest like this."

Hercules ground his teeth. He knew the man believed his own words. There was only one problem. "Nikanor, I am sorry to be the one to tell you this ... but no amount of training can prepare you for a mission like this."

Stories of Dodona

HERCULES CLAWED AT HIS massive chest as his heart threatened to leap straight out of him. He heaved and looked around wildly, holding his hands before his face. The moonlight shone brightly, revealing his clean hands devoid of the blood of his family. The cool light drastically contrasted with the amber firelight he'd just seen in his nightmare.

He pushed himself away from the tree he'd been leaning on and glanced at Liamecles, who slept soundly nearby. Hercules cursed himself for falling asleep while it was his turn to keep watch. How did that even happen? He never fell asleep on watch. An eerie feeling washed over him, and he glanced over his shoulder, peering into the darkness of the forest.

"Are you alright?" a voice whispered from a tree nearby.

Hercules squinted through the shadowy branches of the tree and spotted Nikanor, well-hidden within its boughs. "Fine," Hercules lied. "What are you doing up there?"

"I was on watch."

"I was on wat—" Hercules started to say, but bit his tongue. He regretted the words instantly.

Nikanor deftly maneuvered his way down to the ground and eyed Hercules cautiously. "I see," he whispered. "Four eyes are better than two sometimes."

The Spartan's kindness in overlooking such a blatant falsehood and leaving Hercules some dignity surprised the hero.

"I also don't like to sleep in Dodona. There is a magic to this place … it makes your dreams vivid … almost real. What did the trees show you?"

A low growl worked its way from Hercules' chest to his lips. "The trees showed me nothing. It's the same nightmare I always have. It's never clear, but it's always horrible."

Nikanor nodded thoughtfully. "Sometimes nightmares are hard to see clearly because fear clouds our thoughts."

Hercules grunted.

The two men stood quietly, each watching different parts of the forest. Without prompting the Spartan drew a deep breath and continued. "The trees here have voices," Nikanor explained. "They have the power to give signs and prophecies. Some say better than the Fates themselves."

"I am aware of the stories of Dodona."

"They are not merely stories," the Spartan asserted. "I have heard the oaks speak myself. When my entire squad was slain in a battle against the hamadryads, I ended up lost. In more ways than one. I didn't know where any of the other Spartan groups were. I didn't know what to do. But I heard a voice. A voice like the very earth itself spoke to me. Rich and full of wisdom. It was an ancient oak, comforting me. I no longer felt alone. The oak gave me the guidance I needed to find my way out of the forest so I could go home."

"Why would the oak help you fight against the forest nymphs?"

"I have asked myself that same question over and over again. I often wonder about the magic and the humanity in the creations of the gods. Sometimes, I think the gods spent too much of their good nature on their creations and didn't reserve any for themselves. Many of the Olympians' stories are ... less than encouraging. While a talking oak, a seeming abomination, could have compassion for a man who found himself lost and alone." He glanced at Hercules from the corner of his eye. "You may be surprised at what the trees here will say to you if you're willing to listen."

Hercules let his eyes wander, searching the forest of Dodona for any sign of life. The Spartans lay strewn about, resting. Iole and Liamecles were fast asleep. Nikanor stood before him, but otherwise, they were alone. Or were they ...?

The skin on the back of his neck prickled into gooseflesh. Someone was watching them.

Hercules bolted away from Nikanor. His club swung heavily in his hand as he tore through the trees, chasing a ghostly flash of pale green eyes. When he arrived at the spot where he thought he'd seen them, he spun about, searching for the wretched eyes.

In the dark shadows of the night, he saw little; the moonlight highlighting whatever it could touch with its silver glow. Hercules turned back toward Nikanor. He could no longer see the Spartan's face, but the man's silhouette stood where Hercules had left him. The hero could only imagine the dumbfounded look on Nikanor's face.

Hercules slammed his club down into the duff of the forest floor, scattering moss and dirt and mulch into the air as if the ground erupted. His teeth ground together in frustration. *Where are you?* "Where are you?!" Hercules growled. When he heard no response, his shoulders slumped.

For a moment, he debated whether to return to Nikanor, but he couldn't face the man and explain what had just happened. The Spartan wouldn't understand. He couldn't. Frankly, Hercules couldn't even explain it to himself.

Instead, he walked to the well where he drew himself a drink and splashed some of the cool water on his face before running it through his great mop of hair. He shook like a wet dog, water droplets flying from his hair and his thick beard, but he couldn't shake the feeling that the eyes were still watching him. His shoulders tensed as an uncontrollable shiver slithered down his spine.

A sudden hush fell over the forest—even the leaves of the trees fell silent. His shoulder blades pressed together with tense muscles. Hercules' senses heightened as he listened, hoping to hear his stalker. His heart thumped faster in his chest. The blood inside his muscles ran cold.

The air around him felt stagnant … until it didn't.

Almost as if the forest itself breathed again, Hercules felt the breath like it was on the back of his neck. A voice spoke from behind him.

"Hello, Hercules, Greatest Hero of Greece."

In the Presence of a God

A CERTAIN SOUL-CRUSHING GRAVITY fills the air when in the presence of an Olympian god. Most of the time, they do not reveal themselves in full power or glory, opting to interact with mortals on a level that won't leave them stricken. That had not been the case with Hercules' previous encounters with the gods of Olympus. Nor was it his experience now, as he fell to his knee and bowed before Hera, Queen of Olympus.

"Hera," he stammered out, struggling to bring his fist up to cover the lightning-adorned medallion pinned to the shoulder fold of his lion-skin cloak in a sign of honor.

A quiet filled the forest. No living creature or insect of the night made a sound. That or, as Hercules believed from his previous encounters, there was an aura about the interactions with the gods that sucked all life and noise away that might distract from the gods' desired attention. The silence was palpable, his heart pounding an oddly loud reverberation through his body. Hercules remained kneeling in place, awaiting Hera's words.

After a long while, Hera spoke. "Hercules, arise." Her words cascaded over him like honey.

"Queen of Olympus, what have I done to earn such an honorable visit this night?"

He stood, hardly able to look upon her. She paced slowly around him, the elegant silk of her chiton rippling like waves on the ocean. Her fair countenance, calculating and thoughtful, glimmered with a golden hue, creating an unbelievable beauty about her. Hera looked exactly how Hercules had remembered her.

The goddess had visited him the night he'd slain his family in a bout of madness. When she'd first appeared to him, he assumed the goddess of wives and mothers had come to smite him for the horrible thing he'd done. She would have been justified to flay him where he knelt, blood dripping from his arms. Hers would have been a righteous act of vengeance.

Instead, Hera had been strangely comforting. She spoke to him with gentleness. Though she had given him no answers—for the gods often speak in riddles or enigmas.

Just like that night, so many years ago, Hera did not answer his question directly.

"You travel a dangerous path, son of Zeus," she said, her gold-rimmed eyes piercing him.

"I travel the path I must," Hercules replied, now standing to his full height as though it would show the Queen of Olympus his might and dissuade her concern. He briefly considered asking her to help him remember, but the notion flitted away. Though powerful, she was not the goddess of healing, and Hercules had never been eloquent with his words. He didn't want to give her more reason for concern when she clearly held some already.

Hera, however, betrayed no such emotion on her regal face. "What do you hope to accomplish?"

At this, Hercules paused. He wanted to gain an audience with the gods of Olympus. Here before him stood one of the most influential. And yet, he couldn't bring himself to ask her to help him. Could she? Would she? Would he be able to face the true memory of that night if he were standing in Olympus? What choice did he have?

"I want to complete the greatest mission a Grecian has ever achieved," he finally said.

"Ah, to live up to the name Greatest Hero of Greece," she said, sounding disappointed.

"No," Hercules rebutted gently. He sighed and shifted his stance as she continued to circle him like a cat eyeing fluttering cotton. "I wish to stand before the gods of Olympus. Perhaps someone there can help me remember what happened the night my family died."

"The night you slew them," Hera said evenly.

A barb of pain shot through Hercules' chest, as if someone drove a spear point into him. A shiver crawled through his guts. His fists curled tightly. If Hera hadn't appeared to him that night, he would still not believe he'd done it. He loved his family. They had been everything to him. He still couldn't wrap his mind around the fact that a fit of madness would have been powerful enough to overcome his love for them. But it was the only explanation he had, even if his memories of that night were shattered remnants. "In a bout of madness," he dared to say, doing his best to keep the growl out of his words. "I still don't know what happened that night. I'm hoping that one of your kin in Olympus can help me see clearly."

"And what of your wanton rage upon Eurytus and his house? What of Laomedon and his city? What of the music teacher or the countless others slain by your hand?" Hera seemed to glide as she strode, never breaking eye contact with the stunned man. "All bouts of madness?"

In truth, for many of those incidents, he'd been in his right mind. Both Eurytus and Laomedon had betrayed their word and were criminally corrupted leaders who needed to be taken down. His music teacher had been a pure accident. As a youth, Hercules hadn't completely understood his strength. He'd gotten angry one day—as learning to play the harp can frustrate—and threw his harp. It struck his teacher in the head and killed him instantly.

"I am far from a perfect man. And the blood of innocents is on my hands. However, I have struck down great evils and conquered those who would heap harm on the people they were rightly supposed to protect."

"Hmm," Hera thought aloud. A finger came to her lips as she took in his words. Hercules watched her, worried he may have angered the only god of Olympus who'd ever shown him an inkling of kindness. His breath caught in his throat. Surely, she would have been one of the gods to encourage his entry to Olympus. Now, he may have blown that. Her eyes flitted toward his sleeping company. A strange relief washed over him as her gaze shifted, granting him a momentary reprieve.

"So, you gathered a company for this greatest mission ever. How many will you leave dead in your wake?" she asked, her tone still even, not accusatory.

"Hopefully none," Hercules said honestly. Though he knew it was a far-flung hope, and from the goddess' perspective, it likely seemed a childish one. "I don't doubt we'll face dangers along the way, but I'd like to get into the Underworld and rescue Theseus with no real trouble. If at all possible."

Hera smirked and turned her attention back to him. He wasn't sure what her look meant. Was it pity for his naïve optimism? "So, you go for Theseus."

"He's the greatest hero *I* have ever known. Wisest and kindest. He doesn't deserve the fate that's befallen him."

"Perhaps," Hera said, her eyes narrowing. "But how well do you trust your companions?"

Hercules' face scrunched and his grip on his club loosened. He hadn't realized he'd been holding it so tightly. "What do you mean?"

A crack sounded through the Dodona Forest, the first noise outside the goddess' aura, the sound waves rippling through the air with a strange distortion. Hercules spun and readied his club before him. "Stay behind me," he growled over his shoulder, but realized the goddess had vanished. The eerie golden glow had evaporated, and the moon bathed the forest in silver light and shadows.

Though the wind through the branches of the great oaks was once again audible, none of the nocturnal creatures made a sound. As if every creature had fled the area.

A moonbeam shone oddly on the trunk of a wide oak before him. Hercules knew the stories of the Dodona woods. Knew that some trees spoke, but was that a face?

Hercules stepped nearer, cautiously watching the face. The closer he got to the tree, the more his legs felt like lead, as if his body was trying to tell him something was wrong. He'd learned to trust his gut over the years, so finally, he stopped and stared hard at the face.

An eye blinked open, and the face turned toward him. Its feminine beauty quickly erased as sharp fangs formed into a terrible scowl. Shoulders appeared from the tree as the creature, made of wood and moss, ripped itself away from the bark and fell to the ground. Its body twitched and convulsed as the monster stood. Sickening pops sounded from within as its humanoid body contorted upright in what appeared to be a painful process.

Finally, the creature stood to its full height, shorter and far ganglier than Hercules. Its dull eyes glared at him dangerously. It opened its mouth, revealing jagged teeth, and screamed a wretched cry.

Oh, kopros! Hercules cursed inside. He gripped his club in both hands and shouted, "Hamadryads!"

Hamadryads

SHRILL SCREAMS ECHOED THROUGH the forest, blanketed in the night. Though preoccupied with the hamadryad in front of him, Hercules could hear the Spartans clambering into battle with the attacking monsters. Until he could make it back to his company, he wouldn't know for sure how many Spartans the hamadryads cut down before they were fully awake.

The hamadryad before him skittered through the duff of the forest floor as it lunged toward him. Hercules dodged out of the way, rolling and popping back up to his feet in a rather agile move for the hulking man. The hamadryad threw its head back and belted a horrendous screech of fury, its jagged oaken teeth gnashing wildly. It chittered, and a guttural clicking erupted from inside it as it turned its focus back to Hercules.

The man involuntarily took a step backward. The hideous creature wasn't like the woodland nymphs of other forests—fair and alluring. These were monsters. Parasites on the Selli, the oak whisperers. Leeches, suckling the magic and life force out of the noble oaks. He was not sure what lesser god had created them—surely some vain attempt at creating something as beautiful as the gods of Olympus. But then again, they had created plenty of monsters themselves. Hercules had seen many of their "creations."

The hamadryad's fingers elongated into javelin-like points as the monster dove at him again. Hercules side-stepped the creature, blasting its outstretched arms with a downward strike of his club. Splintering shards exploded from the impact, sending the off-balance monster toppling headlong to the ground. It writhed and shrieked.

The ground around the creature rumbled, and the dirt displaced itself as tree roots erupted to meet the monster. The hamadryad cracked and bent in unnatural angles as it gathered up the roots to forge new arms and raking claws.

"Oh, come on," Hercules grumbled as he lurched forward to blast the creature to bits. His club crashed down on its head, obliterating it and crashing through the rest of its body with the momentum of his mighty swing. The legs of the monster twitched and wriggled grotesquely on the ground.

"Alright," Hercules said to himself. "Not so ba—"

His words cut off as another hamadryad crashed into his back, sending him sprawling. The creature screeched wickedly as it slashed and beat at him. Hercules turned and slammed an elbow into the monster's face, crumpling it as he rolled over.

Another of the monsters jumped on him before he could pull himself to his feet. He reached up to get his hands on the creature's head, intending to rip it from its body, only to find his arms were struggling against roots, wrapping around him and clinging to him tightly. Another root clamped over his neck.

Hercules' eyes bulged. *Not again. What's with them always going for the throat?*

The hamadryad shook madly atop him—unabashed, animalistic glee at its near victory. Its moldy breath heaved on Hercules' face. If his throat hadn't been caught, he would have gagged. The creature opened its jagged jaws, ready to take a bite of the hero's neck and rip out his jugular.

A flaming arrow suddenly blasted into the creature's head, and all the roots that held Hercules retreated. The hamadryad screeched in pain as it clawed at its own face.

Hercules grabbed it by the throat and squeezed. "How do you like it?" he growled as the creature twitched violently. Hercules squeezed harder and harder until a sickening crack made the monster hang limp in his grasp.

He turned to see Liamecles nearby, bow in hand. Hercules gave the man a nod, but Liamecles looked at him with concern etched on his face.

"What?" Hercules asked.

"Your eyes," Liamecles said carefully. "They're glowing green."

Gossip of the Greeks

FLAMING CORPSES LITTERED THE area when Hercules and Liamecles finally made it back to their companions. Unfortunately, those weren't the only bodies that lay dead on the ground. The hamadryads had torn apart several Spartans. Their bodies no longer resembled the fine-tuned warrior physique, but mounds of flesh shredded by the monsters' raking claws. The sharp, broken branches of a nearby tree impaled one unlucky Spartan. Two others were attempting to pull him down.

The scene churned Hercules' stomach. Hera had asked him how many of the Spartans would be left dead in his wake. The hope he'd answered her with had been swiftly eradicated. Smoke singed his nose hairs with an acrid stench. He could taste the bitterness in his mouth.

How could this have happened? They hadn't even made it to the entrance of Hades and they'd already lost half their company. Hera's words tickled the back of his mind. *But how well do you trust your companions?* Hercules shook the thought away. He'd spent years in military campaigns when he was younger. He knew they had to trust each other. If they didn't, the enemy would conquer them with ease while they squabbled amongst themselves. But she was a goddess of Olympus. What insight did she have that Hercules lacked?

Out of the corner of his eye, he saw Iole helping Nikanor drag another Spartan toward a row of those who'd fallen. A twinge of doubt entered his mind. Hadn't Nikanor said he'd been to Dodona before? Hadn't he said the trees spoke to him? How had he been the lone survivor of his band? Had he lured Hercules and all the others into a trap?

Hercules brushed past Liamecles, who hovered nearby, watching him warily. He stormed over to Iole and Nikanor, just as the man was thanking her for her help. Hercules pushed the man's shoulder, sending him toppling to the ground several feet away. Nearby Spartans slid into ready stances, aiming their spears at the hero.

"Hercules, what are you doing?" Iole cried, grabbing at his arm.

"What am *I* doing? I want to know what *he* is doing!" Hercules shouted.

"What are you talking about?" Iole pleaded. She turned to Liamecles for an answer, but the man's concerned look forced her to back away from Hercules.

"I do not understand." Nikanor brushed at his wool chiton, smoothing it quickly.

"There's something I don't understand either," Hercules spat. "You."

Nikanor stood like a statue. If the hero's words confused him, Hercules could not tell. His face only showed a searching stare.

"How were you the only one of your group to survive? Why would the oaks speak to you?" Hercules asked.

"You saw how dangerous the hamadryads are. Look around," Nikanor said, waving a hand over the area. His reaction slowed as his eyes landed on the fallen Spartans next to him. "And the oaks ...

the Selli are compassionate. They have the wisdom of hundreds of years, maybe even thousands. They saw me alone and scared, and they wanted to help me."

"So you could find other fools and lead them into Dodona as a sacrifice to the hamadryads?"

"What?" Now, Nikanor didn't hide his confusion. He looked at Hercules as if he'd lost his mind. "The hamadryads are parasites. The Selli like them even less than we do."

Hercules tightened his grip on his club, but before he took a step closer to the Spartan, Iole spoke. "Hercules, what is this about?"

His teeth ground as he tried to bite back the anger rising within.

"I was visited tonight," he said through clenched teeth. The muscles in his arms rippled under the obvious effort he made to keep himself calm. "Hera came to see me by the well."

"Hera?" several of the Spartans whispered amongst themselves. Many of their readied spears wavered and dropped to their sides.

"Hera was here?" Iole asked, looking around curiously.

"She was," Hercules affirmed. "She asked me how much I trust my companions." His stare bore into Nikanor. "It was only after the attack that I really heard her words."

"Son of Zeus," Nikanor said calmly, raising a hand slowly to show he intended no offense. "We are Spartans. What city in all of Greece gives Zeus more honor? Why would we mean his kin any harm? Many sons of your own blood reside in Sparta."

Hercules suppressed a derisive laugh. Yet again, his youthful wiles caught up with him. In fairness, he couldn't say how many of the claims were false or true. *The gossip of the Greeks*... his people's tongues knew no bounds. Why couldn't he have met Megara first? Things would have been so different. Regardless, just because some claimed lineage from Hercules in Sparta didn't mean the Spartan band of mercenaries held any sort of loyalty to him.

"Hercules," Iole stepped closer to the big man, "their honor toward Zeus is exactly why I chose the Spartans for this quest."

"Well, you chose wrong," Hercules spat and swiveled away.

In truth, he questioned every one of them. How many of the Spartans had also fought in Dodona before? How many of them could have a pact with the hamadryads? Which one of them was biding his time to stick a dagger in Hercules' back? Or Liamecles' back? Or Iole …?

Distrust

WHEN LIAMECLES FINALLY CAUGHT up to him, Hercules was already gathering his waterskin and preparing to continue the mission on his own.

"Where in Boreas are you going?" the man asked, quickly gathering his own things.

"To complete the mission. I'm going to get Alcestis and Theseus from the Underworld."

"All by yourself?"

Hercules paused and glanced at Liamecles. "Looks like you're coming with me."

Liamecles let out a long sigh. "Hercules, we have to talk about this. This isn't right. There's something more at work here."

"I don't trust the Spartans," he said gruffly, standing and facing his friend.

"That's fine," Liamecles said quickly, waving his hands in front of him in surrender. "Frankly, they're a little overeager for my liking, too."

"Then let's go," Hercules grunted. "We don't need them. We've managed plenty of quests on our own."

The hesitation on Liamecles' face told him that the man wasn't so sure he agreed. "And what about Iole?"

"She's the one that hired them. She can go with them or do whatever she wants."

"Really?" Liamecles asked. "After four years with us, you question her? You would just walk away without a word?"

Had it really been four years? Suddenly, Hercules' bones felt tired, as if age was catching up to the mortal half of his body. Liamecles had been with him for what, a dozen years now? *How have I gotten so old?* Hercules wondered. Trials and difficulty had marred the last several years, never seeming to have a moment's rest.

"Moreover, your eyes glowed green," Liamecles pressed the advantage while the thoughts kept Hercules sidetracked.

"Glowed green?" Iole asked as she caught up to them. She'd obviously taken a moment to converse with Nikanor before giving chase. "You mean like the eyes you've seen watching from the shadows?"

"Not like that," Hercules rebutted.

"It seemed a lot like that," Liamecles said, not giving Hercules an out. "Your father mentioned to me that your eyes glowed eerily green the night your family died, as well."

"Amphitryon told you that?" Iole seemed surprised.

"Yes, he was the first to arrive, having seen Hercules' house ablaze that night. Said he was sitting on his front steps when he saw the inferno at the top of the hill and came running."

"Enough," Hercules half-shouted.

Liamecles spoke true of Hercules' adoptive father. Amphitryon had always been a practical man, yet he had a great capacity for compassion. Those qualities made him a standout general of his time. The man had a sharp wit and rarely recounted events inaccurately. Let alone one of the most horrible nights of his life. After all, Amphitryon had lost his grandchildren that night.

Hercules seemed to remember Amphitryon's arrival at his house with strange clarity. He had been a babbling fool, kneeling in a pool of blood, unable to answer the simplest question.

"Hercules, what happened?" Amphitryon had asked over and over. "What happened, my son?"

He remembered too, that his father had said his eyes glowed green. But how could that be? Was it some side effect of the madness? How many times had he seen those pale green eyes lurking in the shadows? How could his own eyes betray him like that? It had to be some cruel jest of the Fates.

Hercules flinched as something grabbed his arm.

Iole pulled back her hand. Her brows drew together as she studied him.

Hercules straightened and eyed her, hoping he masked his own doubts better than she masked her concern. "Are you coming or not?" he asked bluntly.

The question seemed to pierce her, as if the hulking man had stabbed her through the heart with a spear.

"After all these years ..." She barely breathed the words out.

Hercules stood there, thumbing one of the intricate carvings on his club. He didn't respond. What could he say? And anyway, after four years of traveling together, she should know better than anyone that his bullheadedness was even greater than Antaeus, the giant of Libya, known to be the god of stubbornness.

"You really want us to go into Hades and face the Erinyes alone?" Iole asked, shifting tactics.

"Bah," Hercules said, turning on his heel down the path. "The Furies won't be able to stop us."

"You were fortunate to evade their attention last time, but that's not to say you'll avoid them again," Liamecles said carefully.

"Plus, you're trying to pull Alcestis from Death. I doubt the Furies will see the justice in that. They will not let you take her without resistance," Iole added.

"I don't trust the Spartans," Hercules growled, spinning on his friends.

"And you trust Hera?" Liamecles asked.

Hercules nearly bull rushed him. "Hera has been nothing but kind and compassionate to me," he spat. "Even in my darkest hours."

Liamecles held his hands up in front of himself. "All I'm saying is that the gods don't always have a good track record of telling the truth."

"I've seen enough of the gods' trickery to not trust many of them," Hercules said. "But you go too far with your distrust."

"And you're sure it was Hera?" Iole asked.

"Are you—" Hercules' rage cut his own words off. He took a deep breath and rolled his eyes under his closed lids. Both of his closest friends were questioning his sanity.

"Hercules ... It's just the eyes," Liamecles said. "I'm worried about you."

"And I've heard tales of sorcerers who can change their appearance. Perhaps a magic given to them by Zeus. Just like how he pretended to be Amphitryon and your mother couldn't tell. Maybe—"

"Stop it! Both of you!" He shouted so loudly, birds in nearby trees fluttered away into the growing dawn. Just beyond Iole, Nikanor appeared on the path around a bend. The Spartan eyed the hero warily. Hercules' jaw clenched. The way the man looked at him ... maybe Hercules was the monster.

"If you don't think we can do it, then stay," he said to Iole.

With that, he trudged onward down the path. The light footsteps he heard on his heels told him that Liamecles was just behind him. The man was swift-footed and had a knack for agile movements. Hercules wondered if there was anything the man wasn't good at. Sometimes he thought Liamecles would make a much better demigod hero than he did. But that didn't appear to be what the Fates had in mind for their cruel joke.

As they turned around a bend in the trail, he knew they'd lose sight of Iole. Hercules shot a quick glance over his shoulder to see Nikanor standing quietly next to Iole, her eyes watching him leave.

Shrieks

DESPITE WHAT MANY BELIEVED, multiple entrances led to the Underworld. Bards and storytellers liked to embellish their tales with a singular grand entrance, describing it elaborately in numerous ways that never quite matched. In truth, there were many entrances, and most of them were dirty holes in the ground, leading to cavern systems and tunnel ways that crisscrossed into the secret depths of the earth. The irony of all the conflicting accounts of the entrance was that the real indescribable part of the Underworld was Erebus, the impossible-to-map, ever-shifting region.

Hercules remembered making his way through the upper region of the Underworld for the first time with great difficulty. In order to gather information on Erebus prior to his descent, Hercules had sought the aid of a man who claimed to have been summoned to the Underworld by Hades himself. The man mentioned that he'd been down there multiple times, but every time he went through Erebus, the area looked different. When Hercules had gone through the region before, he thought the man had lied to him for his coin and given him a bum map. But as he stood in Erebus now, he believed the man completely.

"Which way?" Liamecles asked in a whisper.

Hercules shook his head slowly as he scanned the wasteland before them. High cavern ceilings bore down with ominous fangs, stalactites of every shape and size. Along the sprawling cavern floor, glowing wisps of ghostly figures moseyed along with no apparent direction. An eerie air hung thick in the place, as if unnatural magic constantly hummed there.

"It all looks different," Hercules said. Then he muttered, "The old man was right."

"Old man?" Liamecles asked, though he didn't turn to look at Hercules, mesmerized by the scene before him.

"Erebus shifts," Hercules explained. "It changes. There is a powerful magic over the place. Part of Hades' defenses for the Underworld. If people can't find their way through Erebus, they never get to Tartarus, where all the souls are kept. Where the asphodel fields rest. Where Hades' palace sits among the barren landscape."

"Charming," Liamecles said with a smirk.

"At least there's color here," Hercules replied, pointing at crystals that grew among the stalactites in varying colors and shone with iridescent light. "Once we're in Tartarus, there is no color. Just pale light against shadowy backdrops."

"Again," Liamacles said, "charming."

Hercules shook his head and grinned. This would not be easy with only two of them, but he was glad Liamecles kept his composure.

"Let's get across this cavern," he said.

"Which of the seven tunnels I can see from here would you like to aim for?" Liamecles teased.

"Whichever one leads down."

They worked their way down to the cavern's main floor, climbing and dropping and picking their way through stalagmites that littered the path. It was slow work, but eventually they landed on the same level as the ghostly figures. Up close, the ghastly creatures looked far less human. Long spindly limbs resembling arms were barely visible, but ended in thin claws the length of daggers. Their wiry frames were no more imposing, each looking like a starved ghost. Shriveled faces and sunken black eyes rounded out their deformed heads. The creatures seemed to have bodies that merely ended in tatters a couple feet above the floor where they floated, with no legs to speak of.

"What are these things?" Liamecles asked quietly.

"Shrieks," Hercules said. "Tools of the Furies. Souls that never made it across the rivers to Tartarus."

"You mean, they didn't have sufficient coin for the ferryman." Liamecles' nose scrunched in disgust.

"Exactly. Cheron might seem harsh, but he's fair across all his encounters."

"Fair?" Liamecles whispered with an incredulous pop of his brow.

"He doesn't give special treatment is all I mean."

"I supposed that's true." Liamecles shrugged and stepped closer to one of the shrieks. "They don't seem to be much of anything, do they?"

"Don't touch them," Hercules said quickly. Liamecles took a tentative step backward. "They might not look like much now, while they're dormant, but if you wake them from their trance and they alert the Furies ... Then you'll see why they're called shrieks."

Liamecles pursed his lips and studied the nearby shrieks. The cavern floor was full of them, meandering aimlessly in no discernible patterns. "How do you propose we get through to the other side without bumping into any of them?"

"Very carefully."

"You? Carefully?" Liamecles stifled a laugh. "There's barely enough space between them for your big self to slip between."

Though Hercules grumbled, Liamecles was right. The last time he was in Erebus, he didn't remember there being so many of the wretches. Why were there so many? "Well, you got a better plan?"

Liamecles scanned the scene for a moment. "They don't seem to be going through the stalagmites and pillars. They're sort of ... moving around them."

"They might not look like they have bodies, but they have mass, just like you and me. They'll feel the bludgeon of a club or the slice of a spear, just like either of us."

"Are you proposing we fight through *all* of them?" Liamecles asked in disbelief.

"No. Only affirming they can't move through the stone."

"Right," Liamecles said, not totally convinced. He scanned the area a moment longer. "So, I suggest we stay as close to the stalagmites as we can, maneuvering around them to position ourselves to get to the next stalagmite with as little exposure as possible."

Hercules grunted. It was a good idea. Better than his idea of blundering through, hoping not to touch any of the shrieks.

"Lead the way," he finally said.

"Gladly," Liamecles said and hopped into motion.

As the younger man nimbly maneuvered between several of the moving shrieks, Hercules wondered if he should have gone first. Keeping up with the swift man would be a challenge.

"One step at a time, big man," Liamecles whispered back to him.

Hercules stiffened, trying to condense his large mass to make himself smaller. Tentatively, he stepped between a couple of shrieks that had just floated past each other. He stopped, holding his breath as another passed just before him. Another shriek drifted by, and Hercules followed in its wake as it skirted around the first large stalagmite.

"See," Liamecles said, turning to slap a hand on Hercules' massive shoulder. "Nothing to it."

Hercules grunted and sucked in a deep breath, not realizing he was still holding it.

They tiptoed around the stalagmite, looking for the best position from which to launch their next route to the safety of another stalagmite. Liamecles halted and pushed back against Hercules, who was following so closely he nearly tumbled over his friend. A shriek wafted by, slowing down as if it were sensing something. Liamecles leaned as far back as he could, pressing against Hercules. The ghastly creature's head twitched as it seemed to sniff the air, though from what they could tell of the shriveled face, the shriek had no nostrils. Its sunken black pits for eyes looked up to the ceiling of the cavern as it pondered, a creepy coo rolling out of its mouth.

Liamecles gulped and reached slowly for his spear over his shoulder. Hercules grabbed his wrist to stop him, the movement halting them both as the shriek twitched to listen. They stood perfectly still, plastered against the stone, as if they were part of the stalagmite.

After what felt like hours, the shriek continued on its aimless floating path.

"That was too close," Liamecles huffed.

At the sound of the other man's breath, Hercules realized he'd been holding his own again and released it with a heavy droop of his shoulders. "Too close."

"There are so many of them."

"So many," Hercules said suspiciously.

"Let's just spread out a little more. Give each other more space for quick adjustments."

"Good idea," Hercules said, and before he could suggest he let the big man take the lead, Liamecles was off again. His movements looked to Hercules like a dance, poised and graceful, slow and steady.

Hercules shook his head as Liamecles deftly dodged a shriek that passed a little too close for comfort, slipping into the safety of a large pillar of rock. Hercules stepped out into the path of several shrieks, doing his best to guess their direction. Some floated by slowly, others with a little more speed. None seemed to float in a straight line. Hercules pulled up short as two shrieks slowed and appeared to be determining which way they wanted to avoid each other.

Why are there so many? This is going to take us forever, Hercules thought as he glanced toward the other side where the tunnels lay. He froze, a chill tingling up his spine as he saw pale green eyes from the shadows near one of the tunnels.

"Liamecles!" he blurted.

The man turned around, looking for the shriek that was certainly on his tail. When he saw none, he looked back at Hercules, confusion written on his face.

"There! The eyes!" Hercules shouted. The monster that had been haunting him for years was here. In Erebus! "Do you see them?"

"Where?" Liamecles asked, turning back to see where Hercules was pointing. The younger hero's eyes widened. "Hercules!"

Suddenly, a cold form bumped into him, sending a frozen bolt of lightning through his body, so penetrating his muscles ached. A shriek gargled in confusion, its mouth gnashing in unnatural angles. Its icy breath floated over Hercules and made the hairs on the man's arm stand on end.

"Oh, gods no ..." Hercules murmured.

The shriek shook violently and reared back its shriveled head, preparing to bellow.

Hercules did the only thing he could think to do. He raised his club in both hands and swung. The club blasted into the shriek's head, splattering ethereal ooze and sending the creature crumpling through the air. Its body, however, slammed into another shriek, which collided with two others. Suddenly, all three of the shrieks were rearing back, their mouths wide.

Hercules could see the terror in Liamecles' eyes as he watched the inevitable unfold. "Run!"

A Dark Hole

THE ECHOED SCREECHES OF all the shrieks in the massive cavern sent shivers up Hercules' back as he barreled through the crowd. The screams pierced his ears with pain and resonated at a frequency that made the glowing crystals brighten to blinding light.

Hercules shouldered through several screeching shrieks and swung his mighty club to bat three others out of his way. The growing number of shrieks swarming the area where he and Liamecles fought their way through only added to the chaos. A glance in front of him confirmed Liamecles hadn't made it much farther than he had, but the man was fighting the creatures off with his spear, swirling and raking with the precision of a dancer.

A ripple of guttural warbles rolled over the crowd of shrieks like a wave. *Kopros,* Hercules cursed inwardly. "One of the Furies is here!" he shouted to Liamecles, hoping the other man could hear his warning over the tumult.

"We can't fight them all," Liamecles shouted back. "There are too many!"

Gods ... Liamecles was right. Already, the shrieks were pressing in on them, almost completely halting their progress. And if the Fury got to them ...

Hercules swung his club, backhanding three more of the foul creatures. Two others slashed and clawed at his arms, drawing blood. The ghastly monsters squeezed so tightly around him, he couldn't tell if the tingling on his arms was the trickling of his own blood or the cold emanating from the shrieks.

Hercules swung madly, blasting a shriek with his elbow, its limp form flopping to the cavern floor instantly. He soon realized he was having difficulty moving his legs. Shriek husks lay scattered around him in a mound up to his hip. He was literally burying himself with their carcasses.

Hercules growled, his teeth clamped tightly. He wasn't really sure what he could do as another wave of shrieks pressed toward him.

Several of the shrieks reared back their shriveled heads suddenly, crying in anguish. Flaming arrowheads protruded from their bellies, the flames quickly freezing into eerie ice sculptures. The heaviness of the frozen flames tilted forward and dragged the shrieks to the floor. Hercules didn't hesitate. He heaved his club high and slammed it down on the toppled shrieks.

Cackling chortles washed over the cavern as droves of the ghastly creatures directed their attention to the way Hercules and Liamecles had entered.

Hercules gave a mighty heft and blasted several of the creatures away with his club. As he pulled himself from the mound of shriek bodies and the ghostly ooze sticking to his legs, he chanced a glance back toward the entrance.

Iole slashed through creature after creature. Spartans fought next to her, wielding their spears with impressive form. The rest of the Spartan company, led by Nikanor, rained flaming arrows down upon the shrieks. For a brief instant, Hercules and Nikanor shared a look. Nikanor gave the hero a quick bob of his head. His face bore no smugness, only a genuine gladness to prove the hero wrong. Hercules gave him a quick nod back, before roaring and putting his full weight behind another swing of his club, tearing through a handful of the shrieks.

"Hercules!" Iole hollered. "We'll fight them as long as we can. Get across to the tunnels."

Hercules didn't answer her, knowing it wasn't necessary. "Liamecles?" he yelled.

"I heard her!" he shouted back. "But I could use some help up here if you're not too busy."

Hercules lowered his shoulder and charged through the shrieks.

Together, they battled through droves of shrieks to get to the other side, with even more on their heels. Thankfully, the Fury that had appeared in the cavern placed more attention on the larger group—Iole and the Spartans. Appearing more solid than its shriek underlings, the Fury's horrifying jaw unhinged, revealing its dripping dagger-like teeth as it screeched. The wretched monster swung its scythe-like arms, slashing with unabated rage. The ethereal cloak of shadows it wore fluttered behind the creature with dizzying ripples.

As Hercules heaved Liamecles atop a boulder leading to the tunnel where he'd seen the pale green eyes, the hero stole a look back at their companions. How wrong he'd been about them. Even after he distrusted them. Even after he'd accused them. They'd come anyway, and likely saved him and Liamecles both. Regret pinged within him, but it was short-lived.

A blood-curdling screech came from down one of the other tunnels. Hercules could only assume it was where the previous Fury had come from, and another was about to join the fray.

"Hercules," Liamecles called over his shoulder as he cut down more shrieks. The creatures skittered up the side of the boulder like ghostly insects. "I think it's time to go!"

Hercules batted another shriek, sending it toppling and knocking its comrades to the cavern floor below. If another Fury entered the cavern, it could bring even more of the foul creatures. Iole and the others needed to retreat. They needed to get out while they could. Hercules growled as he watched them fight on. They couldn't hear him from this distance. And even if they could, he knew Iole would fight on to cover his escape. He ground his teeth and turned to rejoin Liamecles.

"Come on!" Hercules shouted, casting one last glance and appreciative nod to Iole and her Spartans. He knew they were too busy to see it, but his gratitude warranted at least that.

He and Liamecles hustled through the tunnel entrance. The one he'd been aiming for, where he'd seen the eyes. Darkness enveloped them as they turned around a bend where the crystals from the cavern gave no light. They hurried along, carefully sweeping their feet to avoid any stalagmites that might trip them up.

The shrieks pressed in behind them.

"As much fun as fighting those things was, it'd be great if we didn't have to do it in the dark," Liamecles huffed.

"Working on it. Grab my cloak. I'll find us a way through."

Hercules felt a tug on his lion-skin cloak, the clear indicator that Liamecles was right on his tail.

Air brushed his face as if the tunnel had a breath of its own. "Do you feel that?" Hercules asked.

"Feel what?"

As Hercules swept his leg out to feel for stalagmites, the floor beneath his foot vanished. Before he could react, the dirt beneath his other foot crumbled, and he fell forward, tumbling into a hole. Liamecles clung to his cloak, but the man tumbled through the hole as well, bouncing off the rocks with painful cracks. Hercules held the back of his neck, raising his elbows to protect his head as they crunched into rocky ledges and walls. They fell for what seemed like an eternity before Hercules crashed into an alcove, his body awkwardly spanning the gap below.

"Ahh," Hercules cried, his club arm pinned on a shelf of rock.

Liamecles didn't hit the alcove the same way and spun past the bigger man. The lion cloak twisted and jerked at Hercules' throat, choking him as Liamecles dangled below.

"Gods—take my hand," Hercules managed to get out. Blood rushed to his face, veins popping out of his neck and forehead while he reached as far as he could.

Liamecles gripped at the lion-skin cloak, attempting to climb, but his sweaty hands kept slipping on the fur. A small crystal in the wall illuminated the alcove with a faint light, but felt horrifically bright so near to Hercules' face. Though he didn't remember slamming against the originally white crystal when he hit the alcove, it bathed the area in a red glow, covered in his blood.

"I can't reach you," Hercules choked out.

"I ... I can't hold on much longer," Liamecles gasped. "I can't get a good grip."

For the first time in the long years they'd been traveling together, Hercules thought he saw the other man's confidence wavering. His eyes bulged, and his forehead wrinkled.

Blood trickled from a gash on Hercules' head, dripping into his eye. *Yep ...* he thought. *Definitely hit the crystal.* He reached for Liamecles. His fingers stretched wide, hoping for any extra length that might help him reach his friend. "Don't you dare let go," Hercules croaked. He wasn't sure if it was blood, sweat, or a tear that streaked from his eye.

A somber look crossed Liamecles' face. Both men knew Hercules wouldn't be able to reach him. Hercules tried to pull at the cloak to draw it nearer to himself, but with his other arm pinned, and his legs barely holding himself up, he had no leverage.

"Hercules, I have to tell you something ..."

"No," Hercules grunted. "We'll figure this out."

His muscles tensed, and the veins in his arm bulged. Sweat and blood dripped down like raindrops, some landing on Liamecles, others disappearing into the black void below. His arm burned with fatigue. Hercules wasn't sure how much longer he could hold on, either.

"No," Liamecles said, as if he had little time. "You must listen. I'm—"

Suddenly, a falling shriek crashed into Hercules' back, jarring them. Another tumbled past and collided with Liamecles, sending him toppling into the black abyss.

"Liamecles!" Hercules roared.

Two more shrieks crashed down into the alcove. Hercules grabbed one by the throat and squeezed, collapsing the creature's neck and killing it. The other lay limp, wedged into his side. *The monster must have been killed by the fall*. He confirmed the notion when he realized the first one that hit him was still lying motionless on his back.

"Liamecles ..." Hercules murmured as he cried.

All those years together, all the dangers they'd faced. He never thought he'd lose his friend. He'd been the most capable man Hercules had ever known. Regret bristled within him like a spiked flower in his chest. He should have told him that—how impressed he was with the younger man. He should have told him how grateful he was for his friendship ... even if Hercules returned it with a lackluster friendship of his own.

Hercules ground his teeth so hard, he might have ground them to powder. "No, no, no ..." he muttered to himself. His nostrils flared as he fought the overwhelming sadness that fell upon him. He lay there, stuck in place as his blood loss made his mind woozy. Before he knew it, unconsciousness swallowed him.

Stuck

His body burned with terror as he woke from the searing nightmare that plagued him. His muscles spasmed, and he kicked and bucked awkwardly. As he came to, he realized he was falling again, having wriggled himself loose. He banged against a jutting rock, scraping skin from his already bruised and swollen shoulder.

"Raaaghh," Hercules growled as he winced in pain. It took every ounce of his considerable strength for him not to let his club go as he tumbled and jostled against the rocks on his descent. As the hole narrowed, he did his best to force his feet downward, preferring that over leading his fall with his already cracked head.

The hole narrowed considerably, and Hercules' gigantic form scraped to a halt.

"No, no, no," he mumbled, analyzing the situation. His lips cracked, the blood that covered them having dried while he was unconscious.

A stone wall pressed against every square inch of his back. His swollen shoulder wedged him awkwardly on the one side, forcing his arm and club over his head. A jutting stone squeezed at his massive chest, while another rubbed up against his cheek. He had little room to move his other arm, pinned as if he were raising his hand to wave at a far-off companion who'd been searching for him in the crowded streets of Thebes. His hips and feet dangled freely in an unseen cavern.

Hercules was stuck.

A sudden knot formed in his stomach. He heaved against the stone behind him, trying to press himself away from the front rocks that dug into him. His body shifted an inch, but no more. Now the rocks on all sides pressed harder against him. Hercules' eyes strained as they widened, aching with effort. His breath grew short and quick. He felt as though the walls were closing in around him.

Hercules flexed the muscles in his arms, hoping for any sort of relief. The act did little good, his fingers wiggling worthlessly. He started kicking with his legs, swinging his hips back and forth, hoping to shimmy something loose.

Nothing.

He gulped down the growing fear clouding his mind. His fingers traversed the rock above him, searching for any sort of hand hold or ledge he could grip.

Nothing.

His chin quivered as he struggled to heave out the rapid breaths he could no longer control.

This is it? he wondered to himself. A memory of the pale green eyes flashed in his mind. "This is it?" he roared into the void. "After everything we've been through. This is how it ends? You'll let me waste away in a long-forgotten hole until my flesh rips away and my skeleton falls into the abyss? I don't believe it! I don't believe it ..." His words grew quiet. "There's got to be ... This can't be ..."

After everything he'd done in his life. After all the trials he'd overcome. Hercules was going to die in a hole in a far-flung cave ... a broken man. He'd never make it to Tartarus to save Theseus. Greece's Greatest Hero would never get the attention of the gods. He'd never get the chance to ask them to help him fix the broken parts of himself. Hercules would never truly remember what happened that night. He'd never recover Alcestis. Admetus would never know what happened to him or see his lost wife again.

Hercules burst into tears, the streaks cutting lines through the blood and dirt on his face. Stuck there, awaiting the inevitability of death, Hercules was surprised to find himself thinking of Deianira and their children. She'd always been more than compassionate toward him. More than patient. Her delicate and tentative smile rose to the forefront of his mind. She had always been a charming and lovely woman. Far more than he deserved.

It struck Hercules as odd that in this moment, she would come to mind. He'd spent so many years and so much energy focused on what he'd lost, he never took the time to appreciate what he'd gained. Of course, Deianira and the children would never replace Megara and their sons. But perhaps he'd missed the fact that they weren't meant to replace them, but to give him another chance. Another chance at joy. Another chance at experiencing love. Another chance at hope for a future.

Had he been so blinded by his past that he missed what could have been his future?

Admetus' words rang hauntingly through his mind.

"We can't get them back. It is the way of things. Instead, we turn our eyes to what we leave behind."

What was Hercules leaving behind? A devoted wife who would never know what happened to her husband. Children with the blood of the gods running through their veins, wondering what happened to their father. Wondering why he was never there. Wondering why he left and never came back. His gut wrenched. He'd been as absent to them as Zeus had been to him. When he was young, he'd often wondered if Zeus loved him. As he grew, the god's absence poisoned his hope into heartbreak. Had Hercules condemned his own children to such heartbreak?

A sharp pain erupted in his lip as the split that had been closed by dried blood cracked open again. Hercules snarled through the pain, feeling as though he deserved it. Anger coursed through him. Ire that had no target beyond his own breast. He hated himself in that moment. Even if he was cursed, how many blessings had he discounted? How many times had he missed the beauty in life, being so focused on the curses?

Hercules rubbed his cheek on the rock that pressed against his face, scratching the tears away.

"Deianira ..." he whispered into the darkness. "I'm sorry."

Suddenly, the surrounding rock morphed, rippling like water and loosening him from its grip. Hercules scrambled, clawing with his fingers, trying to get a grip before he plummeted to the unknown cavern below. Try as he might, the rock shivered and slipped away, allowing his hands to find no purchase.

Slowly, the rock morphed around the man's enormous shoulders, and he fell.

The Boatman

ICE PIERCED HIS VEINS as Hercules plunged into the frigid waters of one of the Underworld's subterranean rivers. His great muscles spasmed at the drastic change in temperature. His mind reeled as he struggled to find which way was up. Hercules closed his eyes and settled into his descent. He'd never been a skilled swimmer, despite the rumors that said he could swim from Athens to Troy across the Aegean. In truth, his dense muscular frame wasn't right for it, and he sank like a stone every time he entered the water. This trait, however, just so happened to be an advantage for him at that moment. He let himself sink.

Hercules focused on the chilling water around him. It rippled softly by his body. His scrapes and cuts burned fiercely in the cold, but were beginning to numb. *That's it*, he thought to himself as he sensed gravity's pull. He reached up and kicked his legs as he pulled his hand back, his other hand gripping tightly to his club. His lungs screamed, looking for air, but Hercules did not know how far he'd have to swim to break the surface. All he could do was reach, kick, pull.

Reach. Kick. Pull.

Fatigue and cold paralysis worked against him, while the lack of oxygen forced a growing fogginess in his head, threatening to steal his consciousness.

I'm not going to make it, he thought as he continued to swim endlessly. A tingle of doubt slithered up his spine.

As he broke the surface, a coughing fit racked his body. His lungs heaved as though they were trying to figure out how to breathe for the first time. His chiseled jaw shivered, sending drops of water dancing off the ends of his beard hairs.

Hercules sputtered, treading the water. He tried to keep his head above the surface as he strapped his club back into the leather sheath he wore over his shoulder so he could swim with both hands.

A low, irritable grumble resounded behind him.

Hercules shook his head, hardly believing his luck.

What now?

He turned in the water to face the faint outline of a boat, glowing with a ghostly white light that emanated from a small metal cage swaying uneasily on a chain. The chain hung from a hook on a post that bobbed with the boat. From the boat, a tall, slender figure leaned against a long oar. His ridged and cracked skin, if it could be called such, had the texture of a lizard's, but was pale where it didn't appear charred. The figure's long black fingers gripped the oar that supported his weight. His face hid beneath the shrouded shadow of a dark hood. Despite the inability to see his face, Hercules could sense his annoyance through his posture.

"Charon," Hercules greeted the boatman through chattering teeth.

"Son of Zeus," the man-creature replied, his voice low and grating like the sound of gravel rocks grinding together under a wagon wheel.

"Thanks for the helping hand," Hercules said, jutting a hand up toward the stony ceiling high above.

Charon merely nodded.

Hercules knew the boatman possessed magic beyond his own knowledge, but morphing stone like it was liquid had not been an ability he would have guessed. He stared at the darkness where the boatman's face should be, wondering momentarily what else he was capable of.

"Could have dropped me in the boat, though," Hercules chided, a smirk lifting the corner of his bloodied lip.

Charon didn't respond or nod. He made no motion or sign that he'd even heard the remark.

The last time Hercules had come to the Underworld, he'd interacted with Charon in much the same way. Hercules would let the eerie silence between them get the better of him and say something sarcastic, only to be met with more silence from the boatman. It had been purely transactional, Hercules handing over some coin, and Charon ferrying him across the deep waters.

The coins! Hercules started. He patted himself down, nearly dipping under the waters as he did so. His coin pouch was gone. *Kopros,* Hercules cursed internally. *I must have lost it in the fight with the shrieks.* But as he thought about it, he couldn't remember if he still had the coin pouch after their run-in with the hamadryads. Then again, it could have been ripped away from him as he tumbled through the rocky holes.

"Listen, Charon," he stammered. "Remember when I was here last time?"

Charon merely stared at the hero.

"Last time, when I came to get Cerberus? Not ringing any bells?"

Still nothing.

"Well, I paid last time," Hercules said. "Probably more than was fair—"

His words choked off as Charon adjusted into a menacing stance.

"I mean, a fair amount," Hercules corrected. "What I mean is I'd be glad to pay you more than a fair amount this time, if only—" he paused, contorting his face and hoping for sympathy—"I could pay you after we get back?" The last part sounded more like a question as Hercules pressed the words out with little confidence.

"Your way has been paid," Charon croaked.

"What?" Hercules stared at the black void of a face, not sure he had heard the boatman right.

Charon's shoulders drooped, clearly tired of this conversation, even though he'd said few words. A slender black hand wafted over the boat, inviting Hercules to climb aboard.

Hercules clamped his hands on the boat's edge and hoisted himself out of the water and into the boat, awkwardly flopping on the dark wood like a giant fish. He scrambled to his feet and looked Charon up and down, inspecting him cautiously. He wasn't sure what the ferryman meant by his way being paid, but how many times had he had dealings with demigods and creatures? How many times had there been some sort of catch? Charon said nothing, and though there were no eyes on his obsidian face, Hercules knew he was staring back.

"How was my way paid?" Hercules asked slowly.

Charon said nothing.

"Okay ... who paid my way?" he rephrased. Some beings he'd dealt with before got so hung up on semantics. As quiet as Charon was in their previous encounter, Hercules thought he might need a different approach.

The cloak around Charon seemed to sigh, sagging in annoyance.

"That wasn't really an answer," Hercules poked.

"I do not like to dabble in the games of gods and their children," Charon said, his voice like an axe blade dragging across stone.

"What's that supposed to mean?"

Charon said nothing, continuing to steer the boat along the icy waters of the underground waterway.

As the boat swayed, Hercules grabbed the post that bore the weight of the flickering lantern. He thumbed the ridged wood, pondering what Charon had said. Was a god rising against his endeavor? Hades certainly wouldn't be entirely thrilled about Hercules invading the Underworld to retrieve one of his dead subjects. He might even be less thrilled about Hercules' plan to rescue Theseus. Rescuing one of Greece's mightiest heroes ... Maybe that was it. Hercules had become renowned among all Greece for his deeds. No one liked Hades. Whether it be fear or outright avoidance, people didn't like to think about Hades.

"Great," Hercules grumbled. This was Hades' domain. He had oversight on everything that happened in the Underworld. If he wanted to, he could send any number of terrors against Hercules.

The exhausted hero wiped at his face, rubbing the grime from around his eyes. Then he saw them on the distant shore. Pale green eyes glowing from the darkness. "Hades ..." Hercules growled, eyeing the spot with rage. His nostrils flared as he thought of everything the god had cost him. Liamecles, Megara, their children. Deianira ... and their children. Though not dead, Hercules had been so wrapped up in this cursed battle he waged he'd lost so many moments with them.

How had he not seen the trickery of the sordid god? How many others had he tricked in the past? Why would Hades' ego not spur him to target Hercules?

Hercules blinked away the tears forming in his blood-crusted eyes, and the pale green eyes vanished.

A snarl rose from the corner of his lip. "Oh, there's nowhere to hide anymore. I'm coming for you."

A Tricky Path

HERCULES HOBBLED ALONG THE bank of the underground river, moving as stealthily as he could muster. The last thing he wanted to do, now that he'd made it to Tartarus, was to awaken the anger of Cerberus. The three-headed, dragon-tailed dog wasn't exactly his biggest fan. Last time they'd interacted, Hercules had choked the creature into unconsciousness, head by head. He'd barely survived the first time, and he was far less battered than he was this time. Much of the blood that caked his arms was dry and cracked now, but he still looked like something that had crawled up from the grave.

As Hercules continued to walk through the lower region of the Underworld, he saw no sign of Cerberus. *Maybe the beast is off somewhere else, guarding another entrance.* Hercules couldn't shake the feeling this was too easy, as if he were walking into a trap. It wouldn't be the first time. While Liamecles had had a knack for all sorts of heroic qualities, Hercules always had a knack for bullheadedly running straight into traps. *But why would Hades try to stop me with the shrieks and Furies, only to let me in now?*

Nothing made sense. Hercules remembered Charon's words, *"I do not like to dabble in the games of gods and their children."* Neither did he. Hercules had not asked for this life. He had not asked to be born a son of Zeus. *Who would ever ask for this kind of life?* The question sounded stupid. If he asked it in any taverna across Greece, dozens of hands would have shot into the air, each of them foolishly believing his great strength was worth any price. *But they do not know the games the gods play. They do not know the curse of being a scorned child of the gods.*

A burst of sympathy rolled up his throat as he thought of his own children at home with Deianira. Would they be subject to the same fate because of the blood that pumped through their veins?

The sound of moaning and despair jolted him from his own ruminations.

Hercules' pace slowed as he approached the Fields of Mourning. People, ghostly pale in the white light illuminating the enormous cavern, folded over in self-pity, crying dreadful tears. Hercules had not been this far into Tartarus but had heard of the Fields of Mourning. It was said to be the place where unhappy lovers dwelt. People who'd been driven to kill themselves by their misery. A haunting shadow loomed over the place.

Hercules found himself lingering as a dark ache washed over him. How close had he come to ending his own misery and landing in this horrid field to pine away forever? When Megara had died, the thought occurred to him many times. But his father, Amphitryon, and the wise words of his friend Theseus brought him back from the edge.

A strange longing overwhelmed him, tempting him to walk into the field and join the mourners. He was exhausted. His bones longed for rest. He'd fought for so long. His bruised and bloody body ached, his legs hardly able to hold up his weight. He was so tired he could cry. Maybe he could wander over next to that woman who lay on the ghostly grass. Maybe he could just lie there for a few minutes, let his tears soak into the ground. Or maybe ... his eyes glanced about, looking for another spot.

A pair of green eyes stared at him from behind a ghostly tree. Rage boiled within him as he shook the fog from his head. The eyes were gone when he looked back to the spot, but the ghostly tree stood still. It was then that his mind pieced together the fact that everything in the Field of Mourning was merely a shell. The people crying over lost loves were merely shells of who they once were. Even the ghostly grass and foliage were shells of their cousins in the forests on the surface, pallid reflections of the vibrant living things above.

Hercules ground his teeth and marched onward.

When he arrived at a fork in the path, he slowed again. He strained his ears to hear something in the distance down the left-hand path. The sound of wretched screams and clanking chains. He heard what sounded like the guttural cries of torture. *Rhadamanthus,* he thought. *Punishing the wicked for all of their misdeeds.*

For a moment, Hercules wondered if he should go in that direction. Perhaps he deserved to be punished for all the pain he'd inflicted on the world. On his own families.

No. He shook the thought away. He needed to finish this. Maybe he could get an audience with the gods of Olympus and speak to them about the misdeeds of their kin. Then he could tell them what Hades had done. He could tell them of the curses that the god had heaped upon him and many others. No. He would not let Hades get away with it.

"Ha!" he barked a laugh that echoed through the capacious cavern. "You won't win! I won't be tricked anymore!" he yelled. "You hear me? I'm not falling for any more of your tricks."

"Hercules?" a voice called out.

Hercules ripped his club from its leather thong and spun around.

Mighty and Brave

"Brother, I thought you were dead!" Liamecles shouted, leaving a woman and limping as fast as he could to embrace the bigger man.

Tears streamed down his face as Hercules wrapped the other man in his thick arms like a bear. Even though his muscles ached and screamed under the pressure, he squeezed Liamecles like he'd never seen a more wonderful sight. "I thought you were dead!" he shouted.

"Mphmm," Liamecles muffled from Hercules' chest.

"Oh, sorry," he said, pressing the man back and looking him over. "What in Boreas happened to you? You look like you've been through the labyrinth."

"It's nothing." Liamecles chuckled, wincing as he did. Blood soaked his chiton, turning the original white to a pure red.

"You're bleeding," Hercules said.

"You are too," Liamecles said with a coy smirk.

Hercules' gaze fell upon himself. His own chiton was brown where it wasn't red and crusted blood covered the lion-skin cloak he wore. The lightning bolt on the golden medallion, which pinned the cloak, looked ominous, smeared into a reddish gold color. Hercules couldn't help but chuckle. He was a mess. Despite being surprised by his own chuckle, there was no denying the relief that flooded him at the sight of his closest friend.

"What happened to you?" he finally asked.

"He was mighty and brave," a woman behind Liamecles said.

"Alcestis," Hercules uttered, sweeping around Liamecles to pull her in for a gentle hug. He embraced her delicately, as if he might break her, hardly believing she stood before him.

"It's been a while," she said in her familiar, raspy voice.

"Longer than I liked."

"How is my husband?" she asked, with a sparkle of life in her eyes. "I asked Liamecles, but he doesn't know Admetus the way you do."

"He misses you," Hercules replied.

"And I, him."

Hercules glanced over her shoulder and down the path from which they'd come. He couldn't bring himself to ask about Megara and the children. He knew they were somewhere in the Elysian Fields. An ache flitted through his heart. Hercules wanted nothing more than to run into the fields and find them. But what would he say? What could he say? He and Liamecles couldn't bring them all back. Escorting Alcestis back to the surface was going to be hard enough, and they still hadn't gotten to Theseus. The pull to see them again was strong. It had tempted him the last time he'd come to the Underworld, but he wasn't strong enough to face them then. Was he even strong enough to face them now?

"Come on," Liamecles said, jarring Hercules back to their present reality. "We've got to get to Theseus and get out of here."

Hercules watched as Liamecles hobbled forward, attempting to lead them onward. He hurried to the man's side and hefted him upright against his bigger frame. Liamecles sucked air through his clenched teeth.

"What happened?" Hercules asked again.

"Cerberus ..." Liamecles managed to get out. "Chased me all the way to the Elysian Fields. Nearly bit my arm off."

He pointed to his side, and Hercules saw jagged teeth marks that had torn the flesh around his arm and chest.

"Looks like he tried to eat the heart right out of you," Hercules said.

"Wouldn't have been a very good meal, I'd guess," Liamecles said with a smirk.

"What?" Hercules didn't understand.

"Well, I don't think Cerberus eats gold, does he?"

Hercules rolled his eyes and supported his friend. "You're a fool."

"I thought it was funny," Liamecles said through a cough.

"How'd you get away from Cerberus?" Hercules asked.

As he watched Liamecles walk with great effort, his concern grew.

"We fought for a while, but I was *just* able to wrestle him into the river. The mud was too slick, and he couldn't get himself back up on the bank. The river carried him away."

"You threw Cerberus into the river?"

"I saw him do it," Alcestis said proudly.

Hercules' mind raced. He figured the younger man had lost the three-headed dog with his incredible swiftness. But Liamecles had wrestled Cerberus into the river? Hercules had used his incredible strength when he'd faced the hound, and Cerberus had given him a good fight. He eyed the younger man as he helped him walk. Yet again, Liamecles surprised him.

Suddenly, another question pricked his mind. "Liamecles, Charon said my way was already paid when I ran into him. Was that you?"

"Brother," Liamecles huffed, "I have no idea what you're talking about."

"You mean you didn't give him extra coin for my passage?"

"I wish I *had* run into Charon," Liamecles said. "Nearly drowned on that swim. It was so cold. By the time I reached the shore, I had nearly frozen solid."

"You swam?" Hercules asked, stunned, remembering how strained he had been just trying to get to the surface.

"Only to the side of the tunnel where I climbed up and picked my way around on foot where I could. I did have to dip into the water several times before I made it to the path."

Hercules shook his head, then murmured, "Then who paid my way …?"

"Charon said someone paid your way?" Alcestis asked.

"Not exactly," Hercules whispered. "I think Hades wants me to get to him."

"Why would he want that?" Liamecles asked.

"I don't know," Hercules scoffed. "Maybe he finally wants to end this game we've been playing for all these years!"

"I …" Liamecles bit his tongue. "That doesn't make any sense."

Liamecles stumbled over his lethargic feet, but Hercules caught his weight.

"Easy there," Hercules said. Concern rimmed his countenance. As much as he wanted to face off against Hades once and for all. Liamecles was not in good shape. He did not know what shape Theseus would be in either, and it was going to be hard enough to get the three of them out safely without riling the anger of the god of this place.

"Alright," Hercules said. "Let's find Theseus and get out of here."

The Golden Glow

Liamecles stumbled and fell into a small cloud of dust. Wisps of white petals floated away in agitation as he tried to push himself up from the ground.

"Liamecles!" Hercules started. "You said you could walk on your own."

"I know. I know," Liamecles waved the big man off. "It's alright. I'm fine." He sucked a pained breath through his teeth. "Just ... just wanted to roll in the lilies."

Hercules didn't laugh. His grave stare bore into the man.

"They're asphodels," Alcestis corrected him.

Liamecles let out a defeated chuckle. "Well, you got me there. I just need a short break. That's all."

"We have to get to the palace to find Theseus," Hercules said. He scanned the man with concern. Under his breath, he muttered, "Are you going to make it ...?"

He looked out over the vast fields of ghostly white asphodels that waved in the invisible winds of the Underworld. Hercules could not feel the wind, nor did he want to think about the eerie magic at work in the place. In the distance, Hades' palace stood proud and larger than any palace in Greece. The palaces he'd seen in Greece were built for kings. This was a palace for a god. Even with the distance they still had to travel, the palace flaunted its enormity.

"You go on ahead," Liamecles said. "I'll be right behind you."

"We're not leaving you," Hercules retorted.

"It's alright. I'll help him along," Alcestis offered.

"Aren't we supposed to be saving you?" Liamecles joked.

"Seems to me you've done your part," she said with a kind smile. "I'm no useless damsel. I can help you, even if you're stubborn."

Liamecles put a hand to his chest in mock surprise. "Me, stubborn? Have you met this guy?" he said, jutting a thumb toward Hercules.

Alcestis gave him a flat look. Liamecles smiled his dashing grin that had won over so many damsels over the years. "That charm of yours will not work on me. I'm way too old for you. So old I died."

"But still as lovely as ever," Liamecles chimed with a smirk.

"You go," Alcestis said to Hercules. "I'll keep this one in check."

"Alright," Hercules said, but hesitated, taking one more look at Liamecles. Alcestis squinted and nodded her head, assuring him she'd take care of the younger man. "I'll go on ahead. If you stay in the asphodels, you'll be fine. The creatures of the Underworld seem to steer well clear of the flowers. Continue on to the palace, but when you get there, stay outside. I'll get Theseus and return to you. Then we'll get out of this pit together."

"We'll be right behind you," Alcestis said confidently.

Hercules nodded his thanks to her, but before he left, Liamecles grabbed his wrist. Hercules spun to face the man, but struggled to meet his gaze.

"Hey, brother ..." Liamecles said with a weak smile. "Be careful, alright?"

A wicked grin crossed Hercules' face. As much as he didn't want to leave them behind, he also recognized that he'd be able to face Hades without having to worry about them getting caught in the rampage. "Oh, I will."

Hercules stuttered into a painful run. Half his body was covered in bruises and streaking blood stains. Every footfall hit the ground with painful jolts that rattled through his frame. *When did I get so old?* he wondered. He ran through the field, asphodel flowers launching their petals in distress as he rumbled past them. As tired and sore as he was, Hercules never let up. The faster he got to the palace, the more time he'd have to deal with Hades before the other two drew near.

The palace, in all its marble splendor, continued to grow in his vision. The enormous stature of the place sent bile licking up his throat. Or maybe he was bleeding internally. Either way, the ego required to build such a palace to one's own glory fueled Hercules' rage against the god of the Underworld.

As he neared, sounds echoed from inside. Joyful sounds of celebration and mirth. For a moment, Hercules' pace faltered. He had expected to hear sounds similar to those he heard down the left path earlier. Screams and tormented cries. Torturous moans and painful wails. But the noise he heard as he ran nearer sounded more like a dinner party or feast.

Hercules' face tightened into a grimace as his teeth ground against one another. *How dare you!* he thought. *How dare you enjoy feasts and fellowship? How dare you experience joy and pleasure while you inflict suffering and heartache on those of the mortal realm?*

His mounting rage nearly blinded him as he leapt up half the wall, grabbed onto an ornamental design, and planted his feet to start his climb. He couldn't believe that he'd spent so long in utter anguish while Hades spent his days in gratuitous revelries.

As he pulled himself atop a wall, he looked both ways, making sure no one had spotted him. A great terrace spread out before him. His shoulders heaved as he took a moment to breathe. A couple of hallways lined with pillars skirted the marble structure in front of him with several openings that led into other chambers in the palace.

Which one? Hercules wondered.

His eyes darted from hallway to hallway, not really sure which direction he should go. He tried to still himself and sense the direction. The sound of party-goers laughing in merriment killed the silence he tried to invoke. *Well, not that way,* he thought, ruling out the direction of the boisterous noise.

Suddenly, a golden glow emanated from one of the hallways. Hercules flinched and pressed himself behind some barrels, worried that someone might be coming his way. He held his breath as he waited for a guard to come. What if it was a servant coming to retrieve a barrel? Hercules slipped his club from its leather thong and gripped it in his meaty fists.

For a moment, he got lost in the carvings that so intricately decorated the club. It was strange to see the artisan's impressions of his own deeds as he sat hiding behind the barrels. *What am I doing?* he thought. His gut had told him to hide, and when his gut told him something, he usually listened. It had gotten him out of many dangerous situations in the past. He tried to explain it away, as if he was trying not to be spotted so he could get the jump on Hades. But as he sat there behind the barrels, he sensed a deeper dread. Something that sent an eerie slither up his spine.

Hercules grunted the frustration away, hit his back against the barrels twice to pump himself up, and turned and launched himself over the barrels to face his attackers.

But the corridor stood empty.

The golden glow illuminated the hallway with a strange invitation now that he knew there was no torchbearer.

Hercules stepped toward the hallway and the golden glow faded away and reappeared at a side passage several doors down.

"Hera," Hercules breathed with a quiet chuckle. "Thank you."

An Old Friend

THE GOLDEN LIGHT LED him through several curving hallways and winding staircases. The farther he followed, the more distant the noise of the feast grew. *Perfect*, Hercules thought. *Maybe I can get to Theseus without being noticed.*

But his attitude changed as the ruckus of the feast faded away entirely and Hercules found himself in stark silence save for the echoing pat of his sandals on the marble floor. The golden light glowed fainter as he moved along until eventually it ceased altogether.

"Hera ...?" Hercules whisper-called uneasily into the obsidian void surrounding him. "That light was really helpful," he grumbled.

He stepped slowly through the utter darkness, sweeping his feet in arcs before him, trying to avoid running straight into a wall. His foot tapped something, and he paused. He waved his hand in front of him, smacking against something.

What the ...?

The thing didn't move. Hercules felt cloth of some sort over a rigid structure. Almost like a strange statue. He crept around the tall, slender object, only to run into another one. This one stood shorter than the previous. Hercules moved his hands over the wiry form. Bile rose in his throat, and he nearly vomited as his hands reached what felt like a greasy skull.

"Where in Boreas ..." he whispered.

Suddenly, flames erupted, lighting torches that lined the walls of an enormous chamber. The torches blazed to life, one after another, suffusing the room with an amber glow.

"Marsyas' breath!" Hercules cursed as the light revealed dozens and dozens of skeletal warriors standing statuesque in columns and rows.

He stepped back in horror, suddenly feeling very much like he'd walked into a trap. Hercules accidentally bumped a skeleton, knocking it over. The thing crashed to the floor, its spear and shield skittering away and hitting the legs of several others who also crashed to the floor. The clatter rang painfully through the room in stark contrast to the silence of seconds before. Hercules' entire body clenched tight. His face scrunched in horror as he waited for the skeletons to react.

To his surprise, nothing happened. One of the round shields spun for a moment, rotating on its edge until it finally vibrated to the ground. Hercules turned quickly, looking for the door he'd entered. It stood nearby, a singular portal on the wall. He scanned the room and found only one other door at the far end of the large chamber.

Great…

Hercules picked his way through the skeletal sentinels, sometimes turning sideways to squeeze his colossal frame between them. He tiptoed, attempting to be as quiet as possible. Though with all the noise he'd already made, it was unlikely his regular footsteps would wake up the sentinels.

He stopped and stared at one of them. The holes in his skull face gave Hercules no indication of who the skeleton might have been, or even a hint of his mood … or anything, really. The sentinel stood straight, not budging, giving no inkling of life. *Perhaps it's a scarecrow of sorts*, Hercules wondered. *Something to scare others away?* The skeleton's face had small bits of what looked like leathery flesh and some sort of pinkish slime covered the skull. *What happened to you?*

Hercules shivered and continued, not wanting to linger any longer than he already had.

When he arrived at the far door, he took one quick glance back over his shoulder. He couldn't see much of the mess he had made on the far side of the crowded room. Something stirred inside his gut, and he grimaced at the feeling. Something wasn't right.

He spun into the next room, shocked to find a long table and three chairs. Quiet and unmoving individuals occupied two of the chairs, while the chair at the head of the table—the far more ornamented—sat empty. He could not see either of the figures' faces, one being too far and the other facing away from him. Hercules moved into the room with caution, a door on each wall taunting him with the false notion of a simple escape.

He slowly circled the room, staying close to the walls. Neither of the seated figures moved. Were they even breathing?

As Hercules made it to the edge of the first door on his left, he ducked his head around the corner but saw nothing other than a long hallway that turned at the end. He shifted his jaw and crept to the next doorway. As he turned the corner of the room, a lump formed in his throat and a stone dropped in his gut. "Theseus," he breathed.

Theseus sat in the chair that had been facing away from him when he'd entered. Hercules sprinted over to the side of the table, inspecting his old friend. Theseus looked pale and gray, a shell of the great hero he'd once known. Sitting across the table was Pirithous. The younger man looked far worse than Theseus, probably owing to the blood of the gods that ran through Theseus' veins.

A sadness washed over Hercules as he looked at the younger man. He remembered him so vibrant and full of life. Now, Pirithous sat withered, his skin wrinkled and cracked. A twinge of remorse scattered over Hercules like a million skittering spiders on his skin. He wouldn't be able to save Pirithous as well.

Hercules blinked the forming tears away, and careful not to touch the Chair of Forgetfulness, he pulled Theseus upright.

The unmoving man blinked, and his forehead wrinkled as his eyes landed on Hercules. "Easy now," Hercules whispered. "You've been down here a while."

"W-what?" Theseus croaked out.

"It's me, cousin. It's Hercules," he said, grabbing the man's face on both sides and rubbing the side of his head, trying to stimulate his brain.

"I-I ..." Theseus stammered. "Hercules ..." he said, moving the name around in his mouth.

"That's it," he encouraged, smiling broadly at him. "You've been sitting in the Chair of Forgetfulness for a while. It's going to take time for things to come back to you."

"Who's that?" Theseus asked, his eyes bulging at the horrid look of Pirithous.

"Don't worry about him," Hercules said, trying to force Theseus to look back at him. The callousness of his own dismissal of Pirithous barbed his gut. But Hercules knew they didn't have the time or the means to save the man. "We've got to get you out of he—"

His words cut off as he looked up and realized a long shadow was crawling toward them across the floor.

A primal growl bubbled up from his chest.

"Hades."

Games of Gods and Their Children

"Son of Zeus," Hades said, his words fluttering with echoing whispers.

Hercules shoved Theseus behind him and lifted his club in front of himself. Hades stood across the room, the god appearing before the hero without the bright golden light of immortality shining around him. Instead, a darkness shrouded him. Shadows grew up the walls like tendrils of smoke. Hercules imagined it was this place. Dark magic thrived in Tartarus. Just like Theseus had grayed and withered, so too must Hades' golden light.

"So, we're finally going to do this, then," Hercules growled.

"And what is *this*, dear nephew?" his tone dripped with sarcasm.

"All this time. All the tricks and games. I'm through!"

Hades stepped forward, but his long chiton only flourished, as if his feet never touched the ground. Hercules pushed Theseus back, keeping himself between the hero and the god. Hades pursed his gray lips. His sharp eyebrows bobbed over his green eyes as he processed the scene.

"I have no idea what you're talking about," he said evenly.

"*Kopros!*" Hercules shouted. "You know exactly what I'm talking about. I'm sick of your games. You toy with people as if they were your playthings."

Hades' eyes narrowed. "And what have I done to you, nephew?"

"Are you—what?!" Hercules couldn't speak. He couldn't form a sentence. After everything he'd put him through. After all the games and sending monsters and creatures after him. After Megara ... Hercules seethed.

Hades smirked, recognition dawning on his face. "Your bout of madness ..." His words trailed off. "You think that was me?"

Hercules slammed his club on the large table, sending a long crack splintering to the other end. "I know it!" Hercules yelled. "Charon said—"

"Charon?"

"Yes, Charon!" Hercules cut off the question. "Even he doesn't like to get involved in the gods' games with their children."

A wicked smile sliced across Hades' face as he huffed a laugh.

"What's so funny?" Hercules roared, taking two steps toward Hades and slamming his club down on the Chair of Forgetfulness. The chair seemed unaffected by the blow.

Hades looked at the chair, and his eye twitched. "Why do you think it's me who's played games with you? You're no child of mine."

"Are you kidding? What does that matter? You play games with everyone," Hercules accused, tapping the chair with his club. "Prime example."

Hades didn't reply.

"Nothing to say about that, huh?" Hercules mocked. "We both know Theseus isn't your son, either. Yet you toy with him."

"Watch your tongue," Hades sneered. "You know not what you speak of. Pirithous and Theseus were plotting against me and the realm I am charged with protecting."

"Oh, I'm sure!" Hercules balked.

Hades said nothing, his unwavering stare piercing Hercules.

"And I've seen your green eyes," Hercules continued. "Everywhere! Watching me, never leaving me be. Ever since ..."

"Megara," Hades said calmly.

"Don't you say her name! Don't you dare!" Hercules spat, his veins bulging from his temples and his muscles rippling with rage.

"Am I the only being to grace this world with green eyes?" Hades asked, slowly walking around the table, keeping it between himself and the raging hero.

Hercules didn't budge. "Don't play coy with me."

"It appears to me that your own eyes are green, dear nephew."

This time Hercules said nothing.

"Kind of a family trait. Do you know how many of us have emerald orbs? And what about your brother?" Hades continued.

"What?" This caught Hercules off guard. "Iphicles has brown eyes. Stop playing games and let's finish this."

Hades belted a rolling laugh. "Oh, I think not," he said, shaking his head. Hercules wanted to rip the smug smirk right off the god's face. "I think this will be much more fun in Olympus."

Hercules growled.

"There is no fury like a woman scorned ..." Hades muttered.

"What are you talking about?" Hercules barked.

"I'll tell you what," Hades continued. "Usually, the price is a life for a life. It's only fair. However, this is going to be just delicious. So, I'll give you a deal. Two for one."

"No," Hercules said. "We're ending this now."

"Are we?" Hades said, his lips curled into a maniacal grin.

"Hercules?" Liamecles called from one of the side doors.

"What? No! Stay back," Hercules shouted to them.

As he turned back to Hades, the god was gone.

"No!" Hercules roared. His breath caught in his lungs, and his mind raced. *Where did he go?* he thought in a panic. "Where did he go?!" Hercules hollered.

"Hercules, your eyes," Liamecles shouted as he drew nearer. "They're glowing again."

Alcestis hurried to Theseus, checking the hero, who still blinked crazily.

Hercules' body hunched as he gripped his club with both hands and tried to breathe. The air grew icy, and a crack sounded through the surrounding chambers.

Oh, gods no.

A shrill cry rang through the room as skeleton sentinels came crashing through the doors.

"Hercules! We have to go!" Liamecles shouted as he slashed at sentinels who raised their weapons to attack.

Suddenly, all the pent-up rage within him burst like a dam, and Hercules swung his club round, shattering several of the skeletons in one swipe. More of the monsters jumped in and jabbed at his sides with spears. Hercules batted the spears away, tearing their sharp points from his flesh. He roared as new founts of blood poured from his side.

Wave after wave of sentinels poured into the room, leaving no path for an exit. Theseus had slain a skeleton and taken its spear. He cut down sentinel after sentinel, his life of training for battle returning to him in muscle memory as he protected Alcestis in the corner.

"We have to get out of he—Ah!" Hercules shouted as another skeleton stabbed him in his massive pectoral with a spear.

"There are too many of the—Argh!" Liamecles called.

No. No. No! Hercules thought, and he blasted another skeleton with his club. The sentinel exploded into scattering bones. *No, we have to get out of here. But how?* He saw no end to the waves of skeletal sentinels. He hadn't counted when he'd come through the adjoining room, but he knew there were far too many to fight off. They were already overwhelmed, and Liamecles had sustained severe injuries earlier. Hercules wasn't in much better shape himself. Another spear punctured his rib cage.

"Two for one ..." a whisper tickled his ears, even over the tumult.

"No!" Hercules roared, but stumbled to his knee. Skeletons pounced on him like a pack of rabid dogs. He roared and fought them with his bare hands, unable to get a good swing with his club. The skeletons cut at his arms, leaving burning streaks of blood that oozed the life force out of him. His muscles grew weary, and Hercules swayed under his attackers' weight.

"I'll do it!" a shout came from the other side of the room.

The chaos halted.

"I'll do it," Liamecles said again through a cough.

"What? No!" Hercules shouted as he watched, helplessly pinned by the sentinels.

Other skeletons moved about, making a path for Liamecles. The younger man moved slowly, mostly dragging himself through the crowded room. The clacking of his spear on the floor rang out over the suddenly quiet room as he used the weapon as a cane. He paused and coughed blood onto the floor. He leaned against his spear for support before spitting more blood out of his mouth.

"Liamecles, you can't. What are you doing?"

"Two for one, brother," he said with a bloody smirk. "I don't think ... I don't ... it's the best deal we're going to get."

"No. You can't. You'll die down here," Hercules shouted, tears pouring from his eyes and mixing with the grime on his own face.

"I was going to die anyway," Liamecles said, pulling away a torn part of his chiton to bare his torn chest.

"No ... gods, no."

"That's it," Liamecles said as he straightened himself. Skeletons crept out of his way, giving him a clear path directly to the Chair of Forgetfulness. "This was never about me. I could never do what you need to do."

"What?" Hercules whispered, unable to find his voice through the knot in his throat.

"You're Greece's Greatest Hero." Liamecles laughed but coughed more blood. "A woman scorned ..." he chuckled and shook his head. "Do you know what scorned means, brother?"

"What are you even saying?" Hercules cried. He pulled at the skeletons, who held him down, but his strength failed him.

"Disdained. Hated. Despised ... Unwanted." Liamecles took a wheezing breath as he reached his hand out toward the chair.

"Liamecles don't!"

"Brother, we are the scorned. All because of the god-blood that runs through our veins."

"What?"

"You've got to stop this," he choked out. "You've got to end this, so our future siblings aren't cursed like us. Our father ..." Liamecles trailed off.

"Zeus?" Hercules spat. His brows knit together in shock. "Liamecles, you never told me."

A wry smile crept across Liamecles' face. "I know. I was just glad I wasn't alone ... just glad to be with my brother."

"Liamecles, there has to be another way," Hercules cried, his mind racing. The man had always called him brother, and in so many ways, Hercules had felt the same, but he never knew they were actually brothers by blood. He heaved against the stalwart sentinels that held him fast.

Liamecles swayed, almost touching the back of the chair. "You've got ..." He blinked as though he were about to fall asleep. "You've got to save them. Stop this ... once and for all."

"I will. I promise. But you've got to come with me. We can do this together."

"I can't ... I ..." Liamecles gulped as his head drooped. "Not ... not H—"

"Not what?"

"Not H—"

Liamecles' hand gripped the chair. In an instant, his body shifted straight, as if he bore no wound at all. His eyes grew hollow as he sat himself in the Chair of Forgetfulness.

"Noooo!" Hercules roared and ripped several of the skeletons apart with his bare hands. Most of the skeletons released him as they created a barricade around the table in the room. Hercules lifted his club and swung over and over as the skeleton sentinels pushed him and Theseus and Alcestis out of the room. The door vanished, replaced by a marble wall. Once the magical barrier was firmly in place, the sentinels strode to their appointed spots in the large chamber and resumed their statuesque rest.

"Nooo!" Hercules cried as he slumped against the immovable wall. His knees cracked against the floor in a puddle of his own blood.

The Fog

"HERCULES!" ALCESTIS HOLLERED, THOUGH her voice sounded far off. "We need your help!" She shook his shoulders desperately. "Come on ... Come on!"

Skittering noises reached his ears as his brain pieced together the scene around him. Hercules shook his head, its heaviness tempting him to loll to the side and slump back into unconsciousness. A slap stung across his cheek, and his eyes finally met Alcestis'. Terror creased her normally lovely features.

Hercules bolted from the ground, lifting his club in his hand. It was sticky with a putrid black ichor, but a river of blood dripped off the tip of the weapon. With the fog in his head and the deep fatigue that racked him, it took him far too long to realize it was *his* blood.

He turned to see Theseus swiping his spear and scattering a swathe of cat-sized spiders. Hundreds more scuttled down the cavern walls toward them.

"How long was I out?" Hercules asked quickly.

"Not long," Alcestis said, holding her hands out as if to catch a swaying toddler. They both knew she wouldn't be able to hold his immense weight. "After we lost the monsters the first time, we didn't make it very far before you passed out."

"I'm sorry," Hercules said, testing a step. His vision blurred slightly, but he knew Theseus couldn't hold off all the arachnids himself.

"It's not your fault." She quickly changed the subject. "What I don't understand is why Hades would send the spiders to stop us when he could have finished us with the sentinels. It doesn't make any sense."

"No. It doesn't," Hercules agreed. He smacked the side of his head a few times, trying to shake the fog and pump himself up. He sprang into action, racing to Theseus' side. Hercules blasted a spider, more the size of a dog, and its black ichor splattered all over him, mixing with the sticky blood that covered his chiton. The black ooze matched that of the stuff covering his club. His foggy mind vaguely remembered fighting off a horde of the creatures earlier, but the memory almost felt like a dream. The spider monsters pursued them relentlessly. Hercules couldn't make sense of it. Hades had let them go, hoping for some sort of show in Olympus. Why would he chase them with such fervor now?

"Nice of you to rejoin the living," Theseus teased over his shoulder.

Hercules spat a laugh. "You're one to talk."

Theseus paused and looked at Hercules. With a chuckle, he said, "Fair enough." He turned back to their attackers and stabbed another arachnid with his spear. The creature's eight hairy legs stretched wide and shivered in a death cry.

An enormous spider, closer to Hercules' own size, crawled slowly among the stalactites above their heads.

"A mother!" Alcestis cried from behind them.

The spider erupted, spraying ichor in all directions as dozens of hand-sized spiders leapt from her corpse. Many landed on Hercules and Theseus, clambering at them with their multitudinous legs and searching for flesh in which to sink their dripping fangs. Hercules slammed himself into a large stalagmite, squishing several of the creatures instantly. Theseus danced around, flinging the spiders he could get a grip on.

While the new baby spiders distracted the heroes, several of the cat-sized spiders drew nearer. A rock blasted into the monstrous face of one of them, blinding several of its eight eyes. The spider elicited a sickening screech before skittering away to safety. Out of the corner of his eye, Hercules saw Alcestis pick up another rock.

A cat-sized spider sank its fangs into one of Hercules' already open wounds. The spider raked his fangs through the tender flesh. A flash of pain erupted in waves through his body, sending rippling through his brain that made him lightheaded. He shook it away as he dropped his club to the cave floor and grabbed at the spider's legs. The spikes on the ends of the creature's legs dug into his flesh, preparing to hold on. Hercules roared, ripping the spider's legs from his side, leaving its thorax and fangs dangling. He threw the legs and ripped the rest of the spider's body from his own. Picking up his club, he smashed through several spiders attempting to flank Theseus.

By the time they finished fighting off the spiders, they were all covered in ichor, but none looked worse than Hercules, who stumbled along, leading the way to the surface. Above all else, he was determined to complete his mission and get these two to safety. Nothing mattered more. He wouldn't let his brother's sacrifice be in vain.

But the fog in his head grew heavier ...

A Golden Chariot

"Go get Lady Iole. Now!" Hercules heard.

His body floated as if he was bobbing on a boat, but soon he was on the ground again. Violent coughs racked his body before someone rolled him to his side. Clumps of blood flopped out of his mouth, leaving stringy lines trailing from his lips. He inhaled sharply, but a sharp pain in his chest sent him into another coughing fit. He felt as if he were drowning, unable to fill his lungs with air.

"Easy now," a friendly voice said next to him. The bearer of the voice rubbed at his back while other hands kept him propped on his side.

"If we don't get him to the city soon, he's going to choke on his own blood."

Hercules forced his heavy eyes open. His eyelids and the skin on his face cracked the crust that had formed from his dried blood and the dirt and ichor and gods' knew what else he'd collected along the way. He realized he lay on some sort of cloth wrapped around two long wooden poles.

"Hercules," Theseus said behind him.

Hercules forced himself flat to look at his friend. The first face he saw was that of Nikanor. "Easy now," the Spartan said again. The man patted Hercules on the shoulder tenderly. Theseus knelt next to him.

"Go easy, big man," Theseus agreed with a kind smile.

"Wha—what happened?" Hercules croaked.

"You came barreling out of the depths of the Underworld like you were being chased by Cerberus off his chain!" Nikanor said.

"What?"

"Strength like I've never seen!" the Spartan continued. "On one shoulder you carried the woman, and on the other, you carried Theseus himself."

"Kicking stubbornly the whole way, I might add," Theseus said with a sad smirk. "After we ditched the arachnids, we got chased by a horde of shrieks as we tried to escape. Came upon them in a massive cavern. Looked like we missed a mighty battle there. Slain shrieks and warriors scattered across the place. Soon as we entered, you took one look, hoisted us in your arms, and bolted. The Shrieks came tearing after us like they had a score to settle."

"My Spartans ..." A wince crossed Nikanor's face. "What's left of us covered you as you exited into the sunlight. The shrieks hissed and screamed, shying back into the darkness. You set the others down once safe and immediately crashed into the dirt."

"We couldn't wake you, so we put together this contraption to carry you," Theseus said. "Takes four men to carry your butt," he said, tears forming in his eyes. "Rather clever thing Nikanor came up with."

Hercules didn't know what to say. He'd been so aggressive toward the Spartan and distrusted him. Even questioned his honor. And here, yet again, the man had proven himself nothing but a friend. "Thank ..." Hercules swallowed the lump in his throat, though he wasn't sure if it was clotted blood or emotion. "Thank you."

He tried to adjust himself, but wheezed and coughed, which sent radiating waves of pain through his broken body.

"Don't mention it," Nikanor said.

"Hercules?" Iole cried as she slid to her knees on the dirt path next to him. "You're awake."

"Iole," Hercules whispered. He found it difficult to put any volume behind his words. She leaned in to hear him better, her hair brushing against the bloody lion-skin cloak they used to cover him. "I need ... I need you to ..."

"To get to Deianira and the children and get them to Admetus safely," she said, nodding her head.

"Yes," Hercules croaked, though the squinting confusion on his face cracked the dried blood.

"You already told me."

"I did?" he asked as he noticed Alcestis walk up slowly to the group. Tears streamed down her face, streaking through the mud and ichor that covered her as well. Her arms folded over her midsection, holding herself comfortingly. An odd wave of relief washed over him. He'd done it. Hercules had saved Alcestis. He'd rescued Theseus. But grave visages surrounded him. Something was wrong. Other Spartans knelt a respectful distance away, none of them looking at him. They sat hunched, staring at the dirt in defeat.

Hercules realized what was happening.

"You woke up a few hours ago and told me to get her and the children to Admetus. He has enough resources to help them start a new life somewhere else. If you just hold on a little longer, we'll get you to—"

Hercules cut her off with a shaky hand placed on her forearm. The act seemed to break the dam that held back the flood. Iole's tears erupted from her face. "I am undone," Hercules whispered. "Take the club ... and the cloak." He pulled it away from himself, the golden medallion clinking onto his chest painfully. He grimaced and said, "That too. Tell them I'm sorry. Tell them ..." He paused, his torso violently trying to get enough breath. "I love them. I wish ... I'd said it sooner. I wish ..." He paused as coughs racked him again, stealing the little air from his lungs. "I wish I'd told them every day."

"Hercules," Theseus said next to him, but it sounded far away.

A blur of motion stirred around him, but his vision grew fuzzy as his brain felt heavy in his skull.

Suddenly, a golden light blazed through the forest canopy. A crashing noise echoed through his ears as his body went numb to the pain that ravaged him. The wheel of a golden chariot rolled past him. Its spokes were delicately crafted and sculpted with fine epigraphs. Hercules' eyes blurred everything but the exquisite craftsmanship. As the light glinted off of the wheel, Hercules thought that after all the horrible things he'd seen in his life, at least he got to see this before he died.

The weight of his eyelids pulled them closed, and Hercules let out a final stuttered breath.

Green Eyes

GOLDEN LIGHT FILTERED THROUGH his closed eyelids and a warmth washed over Hercules' face. A smile tugged at his lips uninvited, but he did not push it back. For the first time in years, he woke refreshed, as if he'd slept the whole night through. His muscles didn't ache, nor did he feel any pain.

Actually … he felt nothing.

Hercules slowly opened his eyes and found himself in a cozy room with marble walls. Thick white furs, softer than any he'd ever felt before, covered the bed in which he lay. Hercules attempted to turn his head to examine the open doorway, which allowed glorious light to pour into the room, but his head wouldn't move.

"What?" he huffed in desperation as every muscle in his body clenched.

"Oh, you're unable to move while Apollo has his healing spell on you," an unfamiliar voice said nearby. "A minor annoyance, I've been told."

"Who are you?" Hercules asked, a growing weight pressing on his chest as he gave every effort to turn himself in vain. "Show yourself."

The woman giggled, and he heard her footsteps move around the bed. Hercules swiveled his eyes, seemingly the only part of him he could move other than his mouth. He couldn't quite see her as she stopped just outside of his line of vision.

"Oh, I'm nobody," she said coyly. "Hephaestus has his tools and his trinkets, forging beautiful things. Everyone loves him. Ares has his toys and plays among the battlefields ..." She paused for another giggle. "I suppose not everyone loves him, but people know who he is. I'm a nobody. No one talks about me."

If he could shake his head, Hercules would have. "I don't understand," he confessed, giving up the strain in his eyes and staring at the immaculate marble ceiling above him.

"Greatest Hero of Greece," she said with a mocking tone. "Maybe you have too much blood going to those big muscles of yours and not enough going to your mind." Her voice lowered as she continued her outward thoughts. "I'm not sure Mother's plan is going to work ..."

The woman paced slowly around the bed, clearly lost in her own thoughts. She stepped just far enough that Hercules could finally see her. She was tall and lean with golden hair. Though her Olympian power was clear, her face shone with a youthful beauty.

"Who are you?" Hercules asked again.

"Oh?" she turned on him with a start, clearly not realizing she'd paced into his view. "Well, that's just the problem Mother has been talking about, isn't it?" She paused for a long while, but Hercules didn't know what she was talking about. She huffed and said, "I'm Hebe. The forgotten daughter."

Hercules stared wordlessly.

She sighed and cast him a forgiving smile. "I'm your devoted wife. I've been sitting here by your bedside, never leav—"

"Wife?" Hercules spat in confusion. "What ...?"

"Yes," Hebe said with another giggle. "My sweet, I was gifted to you as your bride, oh Greatest Hero of Greece, for all your trials and deeds. Aphrodite was rather tickled about the whole thing. She fought so hard for you to be brought to Olympus. Apollo too. He was grateful for what you did for his friend, Admetus."

"Admetus?" Suddenly, a flood of fond memories washed through Hercules' mind. "Alcestis!" he said.

"Yes, so sweet of you," Hebe replied with a wave of her hand. "I was surprised Uncle Hades also agreed to have you brought to Olympus, but then again, no one ever knows what he's up to," she said with a laugh. "Probably why he's my favorite uncle."

"Uncle," Hercules murmured, he was having a hard time keeping up. *Wife?* "But wait, I already have a wife. Deianira. She's—"

"Dead," Hebe said nonchalantly.

"What?" Hercules' mouth dried up like the desert and a stone formed in his throat. "That ... that can't be ..."

"Slew herself in her grief for what she did to you. Covered your lion-skin cloak with poisonous centaur blood. She's probably in the Fields of Mourning in Tartarus right now."

"What?" Hercules' mind reeled. "None of that is true. She didn't kill me. I ... my message ... she can't be dead. This isn't true!"

"Oh, it's not," Hebe said, waving off the notion with her hand. Hercules' eyes bulged in confusion. Were the gods so callous, spinning tales of people's deaths for some sick jest? "But it's what the people need to believe for all of this to work. The word is already spreading all over Greece."

The stone in his throat dropped to his stomach. "What?" More lies, more gossip. The gods of Olympus were no better than the people of Greece. Worse, as they created and propagated their own lies among the people.

"Of course," Hebe continued, "we'll have to finish her before she has time to refute the story we're weaving. Though we haven't found her yet."

Hercules' veins swelled with rage. "Don't you dare touch her," he spat.

"Dear husband," Hebe tsked. "You look worried. You have nothing left to worry about. You can finally have peace. You can finally have rest after all these years of torment."

Torment. The word echoed in Hercules' mind. Instinctively, his mind raced back to Megara and the night he'd lost her. For the first time, he saw the night clearly. Apollo's healing magic was healing his mind and his body.

The sea breeze had blown mist up from the Aegean, cooling that evening. That part of the memory stood in stark contrast to the blazing fire he usually remembered. But then again, he never remembered the entire night. Hercules stood on the cliffside overlooking the moonlit sea. Megara was inside their home, laying down their youngest. Theo always requested a song before bed. Hercules could still hear her singing softly.

A rustle in the trees nearby caught his attention. His adrenaline spiked as he moved closer to inspect the noise. Perhaps a deer wandering through? The boys always loved when deer came by their house.

Instead, two pale green eyes leered from the shadows. Hercules' steps slowed as he peered through the darkness.

"*Who's there?*" his memory-self asked.

Whispers rolled out from the darkness. Hercules shook his head as if flies invaded his mind.

"*Kill them all ...*" the memory whisper said, and a slender hand reached out from the shadows, a single extended finger touching his forehead.

His eyes glowed green, and Hercules watched himself walk mindlessly back to the house. He grabbed his club that leaned next to the door. Megara met him in the hallway, her eyes bright and smile brighter.

"I just got Theo down," she said. But her face contorted as she asked. *"Is something wrong? Your eyes—"*

Hercules roared in his bed. He couldn't watch the rest of the memory.

"Oh, dear husband, it's alright. I'm here," Hebe said, sitting on the bed next to him and stroking his chest.

He knew the rest of the night. He couldn't relive it. By the end of the memory, he stood over the corpses of his family, his past self not knowing what had happened. He slipped back into the memory, and he realized how quickly Hera had arrived afterward.

Hercules opened his eyes and gazed upon Hebe. Her green eyes looked down at him with consolation. *Hera knew what happened,* Hercules thought. *She knew what happened and showed him mercy, because it was her daughter who'd cursed him.*

"You!" Hercules growled. The venom with which his voice bit made Hebe pull away from him. "You did this. You cursed me! It's been you all along."

"What are you talking about?" Hebe asked curiously.

"You were the eyes that followed my every move. You were the one that placed the bouts of madness on me when my guard was down. You are responsible for the death of my family!" Hercules roared.

Hebe stepped away from the bed, drawing her hands in close to her breast.

"She isn't," a familiar voice came from the door.

Hercules' glare shot toward the door.

Greatest Hero of

Greece

"GREATEST HERO OF GREECE," Hera said with a sigh, shaking her head as she stepped into the room. "How can one so foolish have made it to this point?"

Hera stepped over to Hebe and pulled her close for a hug, stroking her daughter's hair with affection.

"Hera," Hercules breathed a sigh of relief, his muscles bulged but he still couldn't move. "Can you help me? Apollo's magic has me stuck here. Paralyzed."

"I won't be doing that," Hera said, pressing her lips together with a strange look.

"What?" Hercules said. "If you could help me, I'm sure we can sort this all out. I can talk to my father, Zeus, and—"

Hera scoffed at the mention of his father. "Yes," she said with a slow nod. "My husband is rather fond of the honor I've conjured for you."

Hercules didn't respond. Confusion slithered through his mind.

Hera inhaled and let out a sharp sigh as she stepped toward him. "Do you know what it is like to be the goddess of all wives and mothers?"

Hercules didn't, but he had a strange feeling she wasn't really asking.

"To be the goddess of all wives and mothers," Hera continued, "and hear the prayers of women who desperately seek my help with their philandering husbands? Or hear the prayers of mothers who want nothing more than their children to succeed? They want their children to be loved. They want their children to be recognized for what they see in them." Her hand reached out and gripped Hebe's.

"And yet," Hera continued as she stepped closer to the bed. This was the first time Hercules had ever seen her without her godly ethereal glow. Her green eyes locked with his own. "I struggle with the same things. My husband, the mightiest god of Olympus, sows his oats wherever he pleases, and his offspring rise to be heroes among the Greeks. And how stubborn his spawn can be. You have overcome everything I've thrown at you. Become the Greatest Hero of Greece even."

"You," Hercules choked out.

A smile slipped across her face, and she closed her eyes and nodded. "Yes, me."

"How could you ...?" Hercules couldn't even finish the thought, his eyes glossing.

"There's nothing a mother wouldn't do for her own children," she hissed at him. "Her rightful children. You are just another one of my husband's illegitimate monstrosities. Nothing more than a thorn in my side. I've destroyed many before you, and I will destroy many after you. I will continue to devastate the illegitimate bloodlines until none remain. Even if I must hunt them for eternity."

A weak laugh escaped Hercules' lips, surprising him and the two goddesses in the room. "You may destroy us, but we won't be forgotten. People may remember us as legend and myth, but the world will always know that Zeus' love was never solely yours."

"True enough," Hera said. The way she ceded to his words so quickly shot a pang of dread through his gut. "You have made quite the name for yourself. Truly, you've surprised me. Unfortunately, many of your stories cannot be rewritten, as they're too widely known. It's true. But we can use that. This is the part of the story we will get to write. When everyone looks to the heavens to see you, they'll utter the name of Hebe, devoted goddess wife of the Greatest Hero of Greece. The prize for all his valiant deeds. Her beauty and wonder will be renowned. The prize that only the greatest hero the world has ever known could win."

Hercules' eyes flicked to Hebe. Though beautiful, she seemed meek in the presence of her mother. Hebe couldn't meet his gaze.

"You won't get away with this," Hercules spat at Hera. "As soon as I'm healed, I'll talk to my father and—"

"Oh," Hera said with a chuckle, eerily similar to that of her daughter's. "You have no idea what I can get away with. I have power in all the realms, even to the depths of Hades. You think it was him who convinced those spider mothers to burst open and release their babies? You think Zeus has power here? Even now, Zeus isn't in Olympus. Probably off on one of his dalliances, tricking yet another young woman with his charisma. He was happy to hear my proposal to honor you and bade me see it done."

Hercules blinked in rapid succession, trying to gather her meaning.

"Unfortunately, this is where your story ends. You are right, people will never forget you. I plan to place you amongst the stars. A constellation that reminds people of the Greatest Hero of Greece, the one who won the hand of Hebe."

"Wait—" Hercules said, but his words choked off as a tingling crawled up his body from his feet. Pressure built as the tingling moved up his legs.

Hera stepped back and flung her arm wide, sending the furs flying and revealing Hercules' paralyzed form. Radiant light climbed up his mid-section, slowly devouring his body, leaving nothing but the light in its wake.

Suddenly, Hercules could move his arms, and Hera laughed. A cruel joke, allowing him to wriggle helplessly as he pawed at the light crawling up his torso. The white light stuck to his fingers and crawled up his arm, light tendrils reaching and moving like spider legs. "Wait …" Hercules gasped as the light crawled up his neck and devoured his head.

He lay there in the bed, a beacon of pure light. He felt nothing but a horrid tug, as though his light body was attempting to tear itself apart. Though he didn't know how he saw her, a wicked grin hung under Hera's pale green eyes as she watched.

A sudden crack like thunder boomed and his light body ripped into fifteen orbs.

Hera swirled her hand, and the orbs flew out the door and launched into the sky.

Epilogue

IOLE'S EYES GLITTERED, REFLECTING the stars as she stared up into the night sky. Far above her sprawled the newly placed Hercules constellation. She'd heard the story. Everyone had. Hercules had been taken to Olympus and honored for his mighty deeds. He'd been given Hebe, the daughter of Zeus and Hera, as a devoted bride.

Iole gnawed at the inside of her cheek. She couldn't help but wonder at the validity of the stories. Perhaps they were just that: stories. The warrior princess couldn't reconcile the stories with what Hercules had said before Hera came with Apollo on the chariot to the forest that day. Iole had always known him as a serious man. To a fault. Many times, too serious. But there is a forging that happens between warriors who share the heat of battle with one another. She knew him. And she knew he was desperate to keep his family safe.

That's why she hadn't left them yet.

"You know," Deianira said quietly as she stepped next to Iole, "when I look at those stars, I wonder if he had a choice in the matter."

A smirk spread over Iole's face. "I know what you mean."

"My husband was a restless man. Never could keep his feet in one place."

"He always had unfinished business to take care of," Iole said with a shrug, but paused. The thought made her realize she was taking care of that unfinished business of protecting his family. Being laid up in the stars to rest for eternity would not have been his choice. An eerie feeling clambered up her spine. "You should go inside and get some rest."

"You worry too much," Deianira said. "The most consequential thing about our family was that Hercules was my husband. Now, we're nobodies. Not a soul knows who we are here. No one is worried about us."

"I wouldn't be so sure."

"Iole, you've done enough," Deianira said, placing a tender hand on the woman's shoulder. "Look at this. You found us a beautiful place to live out our days in peace where no one knows us."

Iole looked at the place as Deianira waved her hand, indicating the beautiful home. It was no palace, but it was built well with cut stone, covered in plaster, and protected by tile roofing. A fine home for a family. The sound of the sea crashing against the rocks in the distance created a pleasant atmosphere. Fog from the sea cooled the mornings. The Ionian Sea, Iole reminded herself.

Admetus had been more than generous. In his overjoyed state, he nearly packed up his own home and moved Alcestis and himself with the family. Instead, he funded the entire voyage and the purchase of the new home for Hercules' family. Iole and Nikanor had accompanied the family and gotten them as far away from Greece as possible. Naxos was a growing town on the island of Sicilia, and Magna Graecia was burgeoning with new colonies. Without sticking the family in the barbaric lands of a new world, this was the farthest they could move them.

"You don't have to stand guard over us anymore. You've done more than anyone could ever ask," Deianira said. "We'll be able to live quietly here. You've given us a fresh start. I can never thank you enough." She paused and stared up into the night sky. "And I'm sure my husband would say the same."

Iole's gaze lifted heavenward again.

"Plus, you've got a life of your own to live," Deianira added.

"Finally got little Hylas down!" Nikanor said with a victorious laugh as he exited the home to join the women. "That kid has more fire in him than Hephaestus' forge!" The handsome man paused with a goofy grin under the stares of the two women. "What? Did I miss something?"

"No," Deianira said quickly, and nudged Iole with her elbow. "Just proving my point." She strode past the man and patted him on the shoulder before she faked a yawn and stretched. She turned a scandalous leer toward Iole and said, "I was just heading to bed. Goodni-iiight."

Iole rolled her eyes.

"What was that all about?" Nikanor asked as he stepped closer to her.

Iole shook her head. "I have no idea."

"Huh."

"You've grown rather fond of Hylas."

"Ah," Nikanor waved it off with a chuckle. "The boy is a lot like I was when I was his age. He's going to get himself into a lot of trouble."

"Hopefully not too much," Iole said, worry lacing her words.

Nikanor chuckled. "No. Hopefully. But he could grow up to be a mighty warrior. Maybe not as mighty as the Greatest Hero of Greece, but respectable like me."

"Respectable," Iole feigned disbelief.

"Hey, now ..."

Iole smiled, her brilliant white teeth catching the moon's glow.

"You want to put that warrior prowess to the test?" she asked.

"Oh," Nikanor said excitedly. "Ready for another sparring match, are we? You know you only won the last one because I slipped on gravel."

"Ha!" Iole barked a laugh. "You mean the last four times. Do you have excuses for all of them?"

Nikanor breathed in and raised his fingers as if he were about to list off the various reasons for the defeats, but Iole cut him off.

"Besides, that's not what I have in mind."

"Oh, really?" Nikanor asked, now popping an eyebrow at her curiously.

"Now that Deianira and the children are safe, I want to go back and talk with Theseus. By now, his memory has to be rejuvenated. We missed something while they were in Tartarus. I want to know what."

"Okay ..." Nikanor said slowly.

"Then I want to go get Liamecles back."

A pregnant pause lingered between them.

"So ..." Nikanor hemmed. "You and Liamecles ...?"

Iole rolled her eyes again. "Don't be *ilithios*," she said. She grabbed the fabric of his chiton at the chest and pulled him in for a long kiss.

When they finally pulled apart, Nikanor bobbed his brows and said, "I've wanted to kiss you from the day we first met."

Iole huffed a laugh and shook her head. She patted him on the chest and said, "Alright, Cupid. Settle down."

Nikanor shrugged bashfully.

"All I'm saying is that if Hercules were still here, there's no way he would leave Liamecles down in Tartarus."

"I did not know him long, but I have no doubt you are right," Nikanor agreed.

"I just have this strange feeling that this isn't over," Iole said, looking out to the forest limned with the silver light of the moon. The trees swayed easily, enjoying the breeze that rolled off the sea.

"Then we'll finish it together," Nikanor promised.

The night grew late, and the journey that lay before them would prove treacherous. They were going to need all the rest they could get. Before reentering the house for the evening, Iole and Nikanor shared one more secret kiss.

But the kiss was not so secret …

In the shadow of the woods that surrounded the small home, pale green eyes watched with great interest.

Glossary

CHARACTER NAME PRONUNCIATION

Admetus [ad-mee-tuhs]

Alcestis [al-kes-tis]

Deianira [dee-yuh-nahy-ruh]

Hercules [hur-kyuh-leez]

Iole [eye-oh-lay]

Liamecles [lee-am-eh-cleez]

Nikanor [neye-can-or]

Theseus [thee-see-uhs]

Twelve Great Gods of Olympus

Aphrodite [af-ruh-dahy-tee] – goddess of love and beauty

Apollo [uh-pol-oh] – god of light, healing, and music

Ares [air-eez] – god of war

Artemis [ahr-tuh-mis] – goddess huntress and of the dark moon

Athena [uh-thee-nuh] – goddess of wisdom, fertility, and useful arts

Hades [hey-deez] – god of the underworld, presider over the spirits of the dead

Hephaestus [hi-fes-tuhs] – god of fire, metalworking, and handicraft

Hera [her-*uh*] – goddess of wives and mothers

Hermes [hur-meez] – god of the road, commerce, and cunning

Hestia [hes-tee-uh] – goddess of the hearth

Poseidon [poh-sahyd-n] – god of sea

Zeus [zoos] – king of the gods and god of the sky

<u>Twelve Labors of Hercules</u>

Slaying of the Nemean Lion

Slaying of the Nine-Headed Hydra

Capturing of the Fire-Breathing Cerynian Hind

Capturing of the Erymanthian Boar

Cleaning of the Augean Stables

Dispersing of the Stymphalian Birds

Wrangling of the Cretan Bull

Dispersing of the Man-Eating Mares of Diomedes

Acquiring the Girdle of Hippolyta

Acquiring the Cattle of the Three-headed Giant, Geryon

Collecting the Golden Apples of Hesperides

Capturing of the Three-Headed Hound, Cerberus

<u>Miscellaneous</u>

Boreas [bawr-ee-uhs] – the North Winds

Charon [kair-uhn] – ferryman who conveyed the souls of the dead across the Styx

Chiton [kahyt-n] – a gown or tunic, with or without sleeves, worn in ancient Greece

Dodona [duh-doh-nuh] – a forested region of Greece, famously home to the talking oaks

Erebus [er-uh-buhs] and **Tartarus** [tahr-ter-uhs] – the upper and lower regions of the Underworld

Furies [fyu-reez] – the three punishers of evildoers

Hamadryads [ha-ma-drye-ads] – nymphs of the trees

Ilithios [ill-ee-thee-uhs] – idiotic, dumb

Marsyas [mahr-see-uhs] – a satyr who lost in a flute-playing competition with Apollo and was flayed alive as a penalty

Olympus [uh-lim-puhs] – abode of the Greater Grecian Gods

Sparta [spahr-tuh] – Grecian city famous for strict discipline and training of soldiers

Twisted Tales of Familiar Faces

If you enjoyed this dark retelling of the *King Aruthur* legend, don't miss out on the rest of this horrifying collection!

Humbug (Scrooge) - Andre Gonzalez

Sweethaven (Popeye) - RJ Clark

Timber Beast (Paul Bunyan) - A.K. Hughey

Alice (Alice in Wonderland) - Audrey Brice

Wish (Aladdin) - Courtney Konstantin

Quixote (Don Quixote) - Stephen Wertzbaugher

Arturius (King Arthur) - A.K. Hughey

Steamboat (Steamboat Willie) - Courtney Konstantin

Strangled (Rapunzel) - Stephen Wertzbaugher

Dethroning Oz (Wizard of Oz) - Audrey Brice

Scorned (Hercules) - Z.S. Diamanti

Check out the entire collection at www.m4lpublishing.com

Join our newsletter to stay up to date with all upcoming releases at www.m4lpublishing.com

Author's Note

Like many boys of Greek and Italian descent, I became enthralled by mythology from a young age. So, getting to write an eerie retelling of a classic Greek mythology hero like Hercules, is a total dream. I would be remiss if I didn't acknowledge my parents for fostering that curiosity in my siblings and me in those formative years.

With that being said, I have to thank Andre and Natasha for bringing me along on this endeavor. As much as I have loved writing horror short stories, spending a prominent amount of my time in the world of fantasy novels hasn't left much room for horror books. Thanks for putting this on my plate and letting me enjoy the thrills of writing creepy vibes.

And as always, more than anyone else, I thank my wife, Brittany for her continued love and support. Thanks for being there when the adventure is easy, and when horrors come knocking.

Enjoy this book?

We hope you enjoyed this release from M4L Publishing.

Reviews are the most helpful tools in getting new readers for any books. We don't have the financial backing of a New York publishing house and can't afford to blast our books on billboards or bus stops.

(Not yet!)

That said, your honest review can go a long way in helping us reach new readers. If you've enjoyed this book, we'd be forever grateful if you could spend a couple minutes leaving it a review (it can be as short as you like) on the site you purchased this book from.

Thank you so much!

About the author

Z.S. Diamanti is the award-winning author of the Stone & Sky series, an epic fantasy adventure, and cut his writing teeth in horror short stories. He went to college forever and has far too many pieces of paper on his wall. He is a USAF veteran of Operation Enduring Freedom and worked in ministry for over 10 years before pursuing creative endeavors full-time. He and his wife live in Colorado with their four children where they enjoy hikes, camping, and tabletop games.

You can get FREE stories at zsdiamanti.com

Connect on social media @zsdiamanti